Something

SENSATIONAL

To Read in the Train

First published by Lemon Soap Press 2005

Something Sensational to Read in the Train gratefully acknowledges
the generous financial support of the School of English, TCD, and the Dublin City
Council.

ISBN 09547650-1-x

Cover design, text design and typesetting by Anú Design
Printed and bound by βetaprint, Dublin 17, Ireland

Something Sensational to Read in the Train
21 Westland Row
Oscar Wilde Centre
School of English
Trinity College Dublin
Dublin 2
REPUBLIC OF IRELAND

For information on the M. Phil. in Creative Writing
visit www.tcd.ie/OWC

Something SENSATIONAL To Read in the Train

Fiction and Poetry from the
M.Phil in Creative Writing
at the Oscar Wilde Centre,
School of English,
Trinity College, Dublin

One should always have something sensational to read in the train.

—Oscar Wilde, *The Importance of Being Earnest*

Staff

Managing Editor: *John Durnin*

Editors: *Brandon M. Crose*
            Kamala Nair

Editorial Staff: *Patrick Finnegan*
                    Eithne McGuinness

Publicity: *Roisín Boyd*

Proofreaders: *Sabina Conerney*
                 Breda Wall Ryan

Acknowledgements

This publication has been funded by the English Department at Trinity College Dublin and with the support of Dublin City Council.

Thanks to Stephen Matterson, Brenda Brooks and the School of English, TCD; Jack Gilligan of Dublin City Council; Brendan Kennelly, Deirdre Madden, Lilian Foley, Carlo Gébler, Éilís Ní Dhuibhne, Gerald Dawe, Terence Brown, Jonathan Williams, and Sarah Binchy.

Contents

Foreword

Writing is a solitary experience, yet when a group of writers get together and simply enjoy and value each other's company, an atmosphere of lively pleasure is created in which practically anything can be uttered and discussed. In that atmosphere, freedom and discipline are close friends. During this academic year 2004-2005 I've had the privilege of listening to vigorous discussions and the reading aloud of stories, poems, extracts from novels and plays that led to these discussions. I usually received the writers' texts on Wednesday afternoons, so that I could read the work on Wednesday evenings and throughout Thursday, and so be ready for the Friday morning classes which usually lasted between three and four hours with a break in the middle for tea, coffee etc. Sometimes, these breaks sparked completely fresh ideas; maybe it was the change of location or the coffee itself, but the breaks were a crucial and pleasant part of our lively Friday mornings.

What struck me most was the interest the writers showed in each other's work while at the same time working really hard at their own writing. I don't think it's possible to teach writing, but it is possible to help create an atmosphere where vastly different intelligences and imaginations can perceive and articulate moments in each other's work which, when considered and followed through, can often change, in quite significant ways, the quality of the piece or pieces of writing in question. It is this ability to listen, ponder and express which contributes crucially to that creative, helpful atmosphere I'm trying to describe. In such an atmosphere, real honesty is possible, and also, thank heaven, real humour. I often reflected, walking away from the Oscar Wilde Centre after these Friday morning sessions, that I was a lucky man to have shared in the titanic floods of laughter that flowed through the room where we all gathered around a table, looking and listening, talking and laughing, quipping and quizzing, remembering and anticipating, praising and piss-taking, questioning and answering, testing limits and tasting intellectual adventure. I often thought, too, of the impact of that intellectual and imaginative energy not only on my own head, but on the heads of the writers whose company and ideas I had been privileged to share all the morning. The best sign of a session or class for a so-called teacher is that unique blend of animation and tiredness that he or she enjoys and endures for several hours afterwards. It is a very special feeling. And it is all, or practically all, due to the writers' interest in each other's work.

Re-writing is a crucial aspect of writing. It is quite a thrilling and enlightening experience to listen, week after week, to new, re-written versions of a poem, a story, part or parts of a novel, scenes from a play. There is this sense of an imaginative creation finding its full, true shape, slowly and deliberately discovering its own inevitable character and structure. And all the time, fresh suggestions kept pouring in from the individual writer's colleagues. This process of slow growth was a joy to witness.

It should also be said that some writers are able to achieve that full, true shape of their work after one or two drafts. There are no rigid laws governing this aspect of the creative process.

The fact that these writers come from different parts of the world proved a stimulating factor in the round-the-table discussions that helped to produce this book. Speaking with different voices, from different cultures and countries, with different accents, equipped with different uses of English, they challenged and illuminated each other, frequently with sharp eloquence, all through the weeks of each term. I have no doubt that in the years ahead these writers, or many of them, will travel very different roads, but will also keep in touch with each other and with each other's writings. It is true that writing is a solitary experience; it is also true that it can help to create, develop and deepen friendships that quite often grow to be lifelong. I hope, and I believe, that the writers whose work I have been privileged to read and to listen to this year will form those bonds of friendship that make both life and literature deeper, more humane and therefore more beautiful.

Brendan Kennelly

Glass

Georgina Eddison

I THOUGHT ABOUT GLASS. Someone had once told me that even after it cooled and solidified, it still held some memory of its liquid origin. Old window-panes were slightly thicker at the base because the glass had flowed down imperceptibly over time.

Mr. Slavinov had also settled over the years. His belly had softened over the waistband of his trousers and repeated squinting at his work had quilted the area around his eyes with deep-set lines. I watched as he raised the cut glass bowl in the air, turning it to catch the light.

'Hours of work,' he said, his accented voice rinsing around the Sunday morning silence of the factory. He had suggested this tour while the place was empty, the machines quiet. I was due to start work the following day.

'There is nothing to beat the purity of lead crystal.' He stopped and, pulling the bowl closer to his eyes, tutted.

'A flaw.' He pointed to the angled spider web pattern at something I couldn't see. Then, lifting the bowl over his head, he smashed it into a nearby skip. The sound exploded upwards into the high vaulted ceiling, like sacrilege in a church. I winced at the noise.

'What a waste.' I shook my head. Mr. Slavinov shrugged.

'The glass can be melted and reused but when standards are broken they cannot be fixed.'

I followed him into his office.

'Tea?' he asked. I nodded. He made it Russian-style; black with a slice of lemon. He handed me a tall, slim glass set in a silver filigree holder. He bent his head over his own glass and breathed in the rising steam.

'Fragrant,' he said.

I lifted the tea close to my face. I never knew tea had a scent, but it did, so faint you had to breathe deeply to catch it. I smiled at him.

'You are learning my ways,' he said.

I looked around the office. His desk was cluttered with paper; busy with designs. I could see that he had a good eye for sketching. There was a small, gold-coloured tree on his desk. From its branches hung tiny oval frames. In each frame there were photographs faded with age; some were of children, some of adults. They looked foreign.

'Your family?' I pointed. He nodded.

On the window-sill were various glass objects. Among them, I recognized some pieces of Murano glass and a Victorian millefiori paperweight. One piece in particular caught my eye. It was a small candelabra, designed to hold three candles. The handcrafted work was finely detailed. He saw me looking at it and took it down gently.

'Nineteenth century,' he said. 'Note the colour.' It was dull, without the bright glitter of modern cut glass.

'It has a different lead content. That's what makes it appear muted.'

It was as if the glass had been overlaid with a cobweb of shadow.

'It is designed for candle light, not electric light.'

He asked me about my interest in glass. I knew this was where I should have impressed him with my academic career in glass design, but instead I found myself telling him about my childhood. I told him of my seaside holidays in Bray, how I had walked along the beach collecting shells and had become fascinated by the small pieces of sea glass tumbled ashore by the waves. I told him of my delight at the man in the seafront shop who sold tiny glass animals that he made himself. I watched him create them in front of my eyes, melting the glass as if it were toffee and pulling it into fantastic shapes; a fish, a seahorse and even a unicorn that I had kept to this day.

I told him that as a student I had travelled in Europe each summer, avoiding the larger cathedrals and seeking out sleepy villages in Tuscany or Provence, where I could admire stained glass panels jewel bright in the coolness of local churches. How I had lit votive candles; not for religious reasons, but to watch the nib of flame brush the chalky walls with shadow while the sun slowly dimmed the windows.

When I had finished speaking, Mr. Slavinov nodded.

'We will work well together, you and I.'

'That,' I said, lying back on the bed, 'is the ugliest engagement ring I have ever seen.'

Miriam held her hand up and looked at the solitaire set in white gold.

'Dad brought it out of Poland after the war. It's a family heirloom.'

'Poland? Jesus, I don't want to know where it's been. Probably prised off the hand of someone's dying granny and smuggled out God knows how.' I made a face and continued, 'Body cavities, usually.'

'Do you have to be so crude?'

'Part of my charm,' I answered, doing that Groucho thing with my eyebrows. Miriam gave me a quick shove.

'Behave, or you won't get to be my bridesmaid.'

I didn't answer.

'How did the grand tour of the factory go?' Miriam stretched her arms over her head and yawned.

'Fine. Your dad's a nice man. I think I'm going to enjoy working with him.'

'He says you're a gifted designer, and that's high praise from him.' She glanced at her watch.

'Look at the time! I'd better start getting ready. We've to meet the Rabbi for the wedding rehearsal at seven. I'm going for a quick shower.'

I watched as Miriam stepped out of her t-shirt and jeans, kicked off her underwear and wrapped herself in her bathrobe.

'Hope the water's hot.' The door closed behind her.

I picked up the discarded clothes. They were still warm from her body. I pressed them to my face and held them as they cooled.

From the beginning, we were inseparable. We met on our first day at college; two country bumpkins, out of our depth and unsure. Miriam learned quickly, assuming an air of confidence that suited her. I was a hick and I knew it. She was the pretty one. I wasn't exactly plain, but when we went out together, all eyes turned to Miriam like the needle of a compass to the magnetic north. There were rumours about our friendship from the start, even though Miriam was seldom without a boyfriend. I returned to my locker one day to find that someone had scrawled 'Lezzer' on the door in black marker. I didn't bother to wipe it off. When I showed Miriam, she just laughed.

'Why do small-minded people have such bad handwriting?'

I dated, too: a blond, thin Law student who dressed in tweed. I suppose he thought it made him look academic. On our third date he told me he was gay, except he called it 'homosexual' in a way that set my teeth on edge. I didn't mind. Physically, he wasn't my type. I couldn't imagine that he was anyone's type. Miriam was still awake when I got back to the flat that night.

'Did you bring chips? You angel! I'll do the bread and butter.'

We sat together on the battered old settee, sharing a bottle of wine. The carpet had a pattern of autumn leaves against a swirly green background. A jam jar filled with daffodils sat on a side table. They glowed like a lamp in the dimness of the room. Miriam had thrown an orange chiffon scarf over the light shade. She claimed it made the place look cosy. It was her only attempt at decoration. There was a poster on the wall that someone had brought back from London. It showed two pairs of feet in different sexual positions poking out from under a duvet. Just feet and nothing else, but you could tell it was a man and a woman. I told Miriam about Liam's confession. She laughed.

'Poor Gráinne, poor, sweet Gráinne.' Then, leaning over, she kissed my mouth and I tasted salt on her lips. Her hand moved under my shirt, touching my breasts.

Looking back, that was the happiest I've ever been. I suppose anyone who was young in the seventies says that. The world seemed to expand right about then. Anything was possible, even us. Miriam still continued to date, and I occasionally went to the cinema or out for a pizza with some 'reject' as Miriam called them. But at the end of each night we had each other and Miriam belonged to me until morning. Then Sam came into our lives. We met him on a Saturday morning shopping expedition. It was raining. Grafton St. was crowded and each car going by splashed us with muddy water.

'Come on.' Miriam pulled me by the arm. 'Let's get out of the rain.'

We ducked into the Dandelion market. It smelled of musk and sandalwood and damp Afghan coats. Miriam wandered around the stalls, picking up silver earrings carved with tiny intricate roses. She stopped to examine a tray of enamelled rings and brooches before flitting to a rack of posters. They were mostly reproductions of Aubrey Beardsly or bright-coloured Celtic designs by some Irish artist. I looked among a stack of album covers. The stall owner sat with his eyes half closed, the sweet smell of pot spiralling from the cigarette in his hand.

Miriam called me over to her.

'This,' she said, holding up a cheesecloth top, 'is perfect for you.'

I took it from her and dodged behind a rail of clothes to slip it on. I looked at myself in the mirror. It was once part of a wardrobe door and it still had hinges down one side. The glass was mottled with age, the corners patterned in silver and pewter like fish skin but I could see myself clearly. Miriam was right. The top did suit me. The buttery yellow colour warmed my skin. I seemed to glow in the depths of the mirror against the reflected gloom of the market. I touched the Indian embroidery around the neckline and stepped out from behind the rail, striking a pose like a catwalk model. Miriam wasn't watching. She was talking to some scruffy guy. He was wearing a pair of brown cords and an oversized ski jumper that emphasized his skinny frame. I noticed it had a hole in the elbow. I called her twice before she turned to look at me. She didn't comment on the top.

'This is Sam,' she said.

'He,' she announced, sitting in the bath shaving her legs, 'is the one.'

I sat on the edge of the bathtub, sipping a glass of wine.

'The one what?' I asked, absentmindedly picking at a broken tile.

'The one I'm going to marry.'

I started laughing until I saw that she was serious.

'Marry?'

'Yes. He's very suitable; from a good Jewish family.'

I couldn't speak, couldn't look at her. My throat closed in the steamy heat of the bathroom. Leaving the room, I closed the door behind me and stood on the landing. I leaned my forehead on the cold window-pane and stared down into the alleyway that ran alongside the house. It was full of junk; other people's rubbish. A small animal made its way over the plastic bags. I couldn't tell if it was a mouse or a rat. It stopped at a pile of broken bottles, sniffing nervously around the sharp edges.

Miriam held me close that night, making love as if she could break and refashion me into something new; something I didn't want to be. I thought of sand and ice, of how both could become like glass in extremes of temperature. It was morning before I allowed myself to ask.

'Why are you getting married?'

'Because that's what I want to do. I want to settle down and have a family.'

'A family?'

'Yes, Gráinne. I'm an only child. Who else can give my parents grandchildren?'

'You can't make up for the war, you know. It wasn't your fault people died in the camps.' It was a stupid thing to say. I didn't even know what had happened to her family. She never spoke about it.

'You couldn't possibly understand.' I could hear the anger in her voice. 'I am getting married. End of story!'

'Happily ever after?'

She looked at me but didn't answer.

'What about me?' I asked. She turned her face away.

Mr. Slavinov greeted me at the main entrance to the factory that first morning. He kissed me on both cheeks in a stilted, formal way.

'I am very pleased to work with the best friend of my daughter.' I wondered what he would say if he knew we were lovers. I wanted to tell him. Instead, I asked him where my office was.

'Follow me.' He lead me through the factory, already busy with workers. The sun through the skylights threw needles of light around the room, hurting my eyes. It was like the ice queen's palace in the children's fairytale.

'You get used to it,' Mr. Slavinov laughed. I didn't join in.

That first day I worked through my lunch hour designing a gift for Miriam. I decided to make a glass paperweight shaped like an apple. I would leave it plain, just a touch of etching to highlight the contours. I resisted the urge to coil a serpent around the fruit. When I had finished drawing, I brought my design to the glass blower.

He was thin and dark-skinned. I showed him my sketch. He nodded without speaking. I was glad. I wasn't in the mood to talk.

I watched as he produced a form out of the 'gather' of molten glass. The heat from the furnace seemed to shrivel my skin. I could feel a light sheen of moisture cellophane my face and arms. He stood back and I took over—placing the tube to my lips, I began to blow. The glass held the shape of my breath and I moulded the soft mass, a thick pad of cloth protecting my hand. I worked quickly and surely, remembering all I had learned. The glass blower looked on, stepping in only once to guide my hand. The curve of the apple took shape and I pressed a dimple into the surface of the crystal, working until I was satisfied. The glass would be left to cool gradually in the factory kilns until it hardened; transparent and brittle, but still soft enough to carve.

I collected it a few days later and placed it on a low shelf in front of the window. It was breathtaking. Small seeds of air lay trapped inside and a thread of molten glass had fallen back on the body of the paperweight. It sometimes happens at the releasing stage, as the glass is spun free. It had left a watermark. Mr. Slavinov would have called it imperfect. I highlighted the curve of the apple, polishing it with a bloom like the first touch of ice on water. I knew she would love it. I held it in the palm of my hand; a globe of solid air, heavy as a small world. I showed it to Mr. Slavinov anyway. He held it to the light and turned it carefully. He nodded slowly.

'It has balance and form. My daughter will see it every day and be reminded of you.' He made eye contact with me for the first time. His eyes were dark, expressive. I'm not sure what I could see in them. But there was something.

I spent the night before the wedding with Miriam. It was her last night in her parents' house. I needed to speak, but the words caught like splinters in the back of my throat.

'Leave the curtains open, Gráinne.' Miriam lay back on her pillow. Moonlight silvered the room, making it feel like we were under water. I undressed, leaving my clothes in a pile on the floor, as if going to sleep were a kind of suicide and that by diving into bed there was a hope I wouldn't surface into morning. I started to speak.

'Shh,' Miriam whispered, laying her finger across my lips. I kissed her, moving my mouth over her skin, my breath seeking the warmest folds, my hands shaping her body. We made love. Once in the night I thought I saw a shadow move on the wall of the bedroom. I raised my head. The door closed with a brittle click, like a tut of disapproval or a piece of glass released from the gather. Night cooled into morning.

I watched as Miriam took her place under the canopy beside Sam and the Rabbi began intoning the ceremony that would take her away from me. I glanced around the synagogue. The movement of the congregation seemed slightly out of focus, jerky; like a silent film that might at any point melt into stuttering flames.

'Don't faint, don't faint,' a voice in my head insisted. Furious tears filled my eyes. I watched, willing Miriam to turn around. Just once, for the briefest moment, she looked back, then turned to face her groom; still as a pillar of salt in her white dress.

I felt a hand take hold of mine. It was Mr. Slavinov. We listened together as the Rabbi ended the ceremony. I looked away as the groom stepped forward to crush the glass under his heel and met Mr. Slavinov's eyes. This time, I thought I could read what they said. It was about loss. And survival. Maybe his, maybe mine.

The Clammy Hand
of Murder

☙❧

William Collinson

THE VILLAGE OF CRONDALL lay in a quiet slumber as the warm, clammy hand of murder approached from over the fields. The last of the drinkers at The Plume Of Feathers had long ago wound his way home and the pub had settled snugly into the darkness. Thus, the streets were empty as the ragged spectre of death entered and stalked with a watchful eye and a quick temper, peering through windows and silently testing locked doors. Eventually, the spectre finds who it is looking for; crouched in the bushes, dressed in black, sweating like a pig in a faulty sauna.

We have found our murderer, ladies and gentlemen, but I'm not going to give the game away at this stage by saying 'him' or 'her.' I know who did it, obviously, and I know why they did it, and frankly I don't blame them. I don't think I could do what they were about to do, but sometimes I wish I could. Could you? Could you look through your wardrobe and select your black clothes, your murder clothes? It couldn't be your best things, or a favourite pair of trousers—after all, you're not going to be able to wear these things again. Imagine going for a drink in a pair of trousers you have worn whilst murdering someone. What if you don't have enough black clothes? What if you had to go shopping especially for appropriate murder clothes? Can you imagine? This is no crime of passion, no drunken spurt of violence.

This is murder at its coldest.[1]

I can tell you that the murderer systematically went through the knives in the kitchen, trying to work out which was the most suitable for the task. First thought is obviously the biggest, sharpest knife, but this is difficult to carry. What about a penknife then? Might take rather a long time to finish him off with a penknife, and no one wants that. Our murderer finds it hard to think about being a killer at all, let alone the contemplation of the act itself. How awful to stab someone and have them still alive when the knife comes out. The murderer appreciated that to kill someone stone dead with a single stab wound is virtually impossible. They bleed and bleed, you know, and whine and shriek and groan and look at you all the time.

Knives make impractical murder weapons unless you are a professional assassin, and as you have probably gathered by now, our sweating, trembling murderer is not a professional.[2] But what other choice was there? The murderer did not have access to a gun, and even if they did, something like a gun is far too traceable in a village like Crondall. Poison? Attractively Agatha Christie in its associations maybe, but what did the murderer know of poisons and the best way to administer them? Strangulation seemed too imprecise, similarly full on battery with a blunt object. Well that was all the Cluedo murder weapons covered—a knife it would have to be.

The plan? Nothing intricate, nothing complicated, nothing devilishly cunning. I once saw an episode of *Midsomer Murders* where a man was lured with money onto some weakened floorboards above some sharp, pointy farming equipment. Who the bloody hell would murder someone like that? What if he saw the cuts in the boards? What if he wasn't heavy enough to go through them? What if the farming equipment merely maims him rather than kills him? The whole thing is an absolute nightmare as far as the practical side of murder is concerned. No, our murderer has a much better idea. Break into the house whilst the victim is asleep, creep upstairs, stab

---

[1] Yes, I know I said the hand of murder is warm and clammy. The *act* is cold, the *hand* that does the act is warm and clammy, okay? This really is too early for pedantry.

[2] Professional assassins don't wear balaclavas from Marks and Spencer's. I think we can all agree on that.

him, leave. The beauty of this idea is that no alibi is required; one can simply say one was asleep like everyone else. And everyone has knives at home, as we've already established, so the method of murder is very non-specific. It could have been anyone.

The spectre of death is becoming rather bored with all this flim flamming. Enough with the bushes already, get on with it! The murderer breaks cover, clutching the knife, which, for want of a better sheath, has been wrapped in a couple of pairs of socks.

I haven't told you which bush the murderer was in, have I? It's not like you could have been expected to guess. Even those amongst you that have a full and detailed knowledge of Crondall can't be expected to work out which bush it was. Crondall's not huge as villages go but my word there's an awful lot of bush, if you'll excuse the expression. Well. I'll tell you. It was the big greeny-brown bush at the entrance to the drive of Critchley House. Not the really big green one on the left, that's actually technically a tree, it just looks like a bush and anyway it's far too prickly. No, this one was definitely a bush. But look, let's not get too bogged down in the whole bush/tree debate, the murderer isn't even in the damn thing anymore for a start. The murderer, the recently bushed but now debushed murderer, is sprinting across the front lawn, acutely aware of how noisy these trainers are being. The trainers were selected because they're supposed to be stealthy, but these ones seem to be all, well, thumpy.[3] God, the left one even has a bloody squeak! The whole thing is descending into farce. Just remember that at the end of this chapter, a man will be lying dead, so it's no laughing matter.

Despite all the thumping and squeaking, the murderer reaches the corner of the house undetected. Critchley House has one of those arc-shaped gravel drives that lots of posh houses have. They're quite effective at deterring burglars (and inexperienced murderers carrying a knife in a sock) because it's extraordinarily difficult to walk quietly on gravel. Luckily for our murderer, however, a plank of

---

[3] My computer tells me that 'thumpy' isn't a word, but that's what they were. They were thumpy. We all know what I mean by 'thumpy' anyway, even if my computer is claiming ignorance.

wood from the scaffolding on the east wing of the house has been left across the thinnest part of the drive that needs to be crossed. This, rather melodramatically, I shall call 'The Bridge Of Death'. Creepily and carefully the murderer carefully creeps across the gravel crevasse.[4] Then the Georgian windows are tested and, sure enough, one of the windows leading to the drawing room, 'The Window Of Death' if you will, slides up easily. What would the murderer have done if a window hadn't been open, you ask? To tell you the truth, I'm not sure, but the point is that the window *was* open so let's not argue about it.

Into the drawing room, 'The Drawing Room Of Death,' and the first thing goes wrong for our murderer. A blue-and-white vase (I want to say a Ming vase but I really don't know what sort of vase it was; a breakable one, that's for sure) fell to the ground having come into contact with a squeaky trainer and, true to form, broke. Now it didn't make an enormous crash—those of you who know Critchley House will know it is carpeted everywhere apart from the kitchen, and what thick lustrous carpet it is too—and vase on carpet makes more of a hollow tinkle than an enormous crash. Still, this is the sort of noise that would normally have had Cobbles, Critchley House's resident Pit Bull Terrier, scurrying into the drawing room, there, there by God, to disembowel anything that moved. But, two days earlier, Cobbles had attacked a young man called Wayne whilst he and his friends sat on the swings in the park smoking funny cigarettes, and Wayne's father had insisted that the vicious hound be destroyed.[5] Another stroke of luck for our murderer. Upstairs the victim still sleeps, several pints in the Plume having had an anaesthetizing effect.

However, the second thing goes wrong at this point. The TV remote has been left on the floor and our hapless murderer steps on it. Now I reckon you could tread on a remote control nine times out of ten and nothing would happen, but Lady Luck is playing a

---

[4] Alright, so it wasn't really a crevasse, but I wanted to keep the alliteration going and that was all I could think of.

[5] Destroyed always makes me think the poor creature is blown to smithereens with some sort of Bazooka, which would probably be more fun for the vet.

dangerous game with our murderer, and the television roars into life. Ideally it would be some sort of murder mystery that started up, that would really round off the whole postmodern irony thing I've got going on, but of course they don't show murder mysteries at twenty seven minutes past one on a Thursday morning. Instead I'm afraid it was Ainsley Harriet that appeared, the decadently wide wide-screen TV revealing him in all his ghastly grinning glory.

'Just a sprinkle of paprika in there, ooh lovely, look at that, super...'

The murderer desperately picks up the remote and frantically pushes the buttons, but to no avail. Upstairs, the rumblings of an awoken victim. Fuck. Fuck fuck fuck shit fuck. *Fuck*. Our murderer thinks of escape. Despite the motive for murder—and it really is a very good motive as I think you'll agree when you eventually discover it—the murderer strongly considers piling straight back through the Window Of Death and legging it. A voice from upstairs,

'If you're down there you'd better hope I don't find you! I'll skin you alive, you little bastard!'

Suddenly the seething, boiling hatred returns. The sound of his voice triggers the same dribbling fury that originally prompted our murderer to go balaclava shopping. The knife is unwrapped from the socks. Here, then, right here in the drawing room, right here as Ainsley Harriet talks about curried swordfish, this is where he'll meet his end. That evil fucking shit-eating bastard will die here.

A footstep upon the stairs.

The murderer hides behind the door.

A voice, 'You'd better run now you little shit!'

The murderer clutches the handle of the knife tighter and lets out a long, shaky breath.

Another footstep upon the stairs.

The murderer's black, long sleeved T-shirt is sweat-soaked.

Another footstep upon the stairs.

'Boil that for just five minutes there,...' grins Harriet.

Another footstep and then nothing. He's in the hallway. He's in the hallway and the murderer can't hear him because of that carpet we discussed earlier.

Enter the victim.

Appallingly, he is absolutely and thoroughly nude.

Even more appallingly for our dear murderer, who I think we've all come to like over the last few pages, the nude victim is carrying a double-barrelled shotgun.

There is a big difference, my friends, a big difference between murdering a sleeping man in his bed and murdering a nude maniac holding a gun. A big difference. Huge. Whopping. I've never had to do either, and I suspect you haven't,[6] but we can imagine the difference. And it's a big one.

For a moment, the murderer contemplates the dreadful sight of a naked old man holding a gun, silhouetted in front of 'Ready Steady Cook,' his horrible old man's penis looking straight into the shadow behind the door.

With what the murderer hopes sounds like a guttural bellow of passion, battle is joined. If this were radio, you'd hear the following:

'Warrrrgggggghhhhhhhh!'

BANG!

'Shit!'

'Ow!'

Stabbed he was, but far from dead. Upon hearing a peculiarly high-pitched shriek, the victim had turned his back and the descending knife had missed everything apart from the leading edge of the left buttock. The shock of being stabbed in the buttock, stabbed pretty ineffectually it must be said, but stabbed all the same, meant that the shotgun was fired directly into the ceiling above the murderer's head. A large piece of plaster bounces off the balaclava as the majestic pair spring apart.

The murderer and the victim contemplate each other. The victim raises the shotgun, ready to discharge the second barrel. The murderer throws the knife at the victim.

As we settled earlier, this is not a professional assassin. A profes-

---

[6] Unless you are a murderer. In which case I won't tell you your business, after all, you know far more about this sort of thing than I.

sional assassin would not stab someone in the buttock. It would be embarrassing. Also, a pro would know that a kitchen knife does not throw like those knives in the movies. You see, the handle is too heavy so it won't rotate properly, resulting in the handle making contact with the victim rather than the pointy bit. Still, being hit on the ear with a knife handle was enough to mean the victim missed the murderer with his second shot as well as the first.

The victim throws the gun at the murderer. The murderer ducks. The gun hits a small table with a blue-and-white vase on it. The vase falls off the table. The vase is caught by the murderer. The murderer realises that it is the twin of the one broken earlier. They were a set. The vase is thrown at the victim. The vase is caught by a somewhat surprised victim and thrown back. The vase breaks against the wall.

The murderer and the victim stare at each other.

They've run out of things to throw.

This was not at all what the murderer had in mind. To be quite honest, the murderer has half a notion to call it quits, broker some sort of truce and walk home. But the victim has other ideas. He is not a nice man. Alright, so most people having been stabbed in the buttock by a masked assassin would be upset, perhaps even miffed or possibly cheesed off. But the victim, feeling the warm trickle of blood down his left leg, is rather more than cheesed off; he is murderous. He leaps at the murderer,[7] tearing with his bare hands at the very flesh that tried to send him from this world.

Again, most of us will never experience the primal spectacle of fighting for our lives with our bare hands. How lucky we are, tucked up in our beds, enjoying the first chapter of a slightly strange murder mystery novel, safe in the knowledge we will never have to scrabble at an assailant's face, clawing at eyes and ears and noses[8] like an animal. It's not pleasant, I can tell you that much, not pleasant at all.

---

[7] The murderer has become the victim and the victim has become the murderer but we're going to keep calling them murderer and victim, otherwise it's all going to become too confusing for words and we'll all need a sit down.

[8] Noses? If your assailant has more than one nose then they should at least be easy to identify.

How best to describe what happened next? Well look, the pair of them are on the floor, rolling around, each trying to strangle the other, occasionally trying to bite each other, which isn't easy when you're wearing a balaclava. As they roll they bump into things, knock things off coffee tables and generally make a mess. In particular, they bump into the table upon which the television sits. This, to revisit an old motif, is 'The Television Of Death,' and every time they bump into the table 'pon which it sits, The Television Of Death inches ever closer to the edge.

Eventually, inevitably, and perhaps with a little push from Lady Luck, who frankly is being a complete bitch this evening, The Television Of Death topples from its table and, with Ainsley still blithering away, falls directly on top of the struggling pair.

It should be noted that the coroner could not decide exactly what killed the two of them. The television had landed upon their heads and both parties had severe head wounds that would have certainly killed them. But of course, the television was on at the moment it hit them, meaning they were also both electrocuted when the screen shattered.

Personally, I don't think it's really that important. The key thing to concentrate on is that they are dead. Brian Fallows, nude occupier of Critchley House and professional nasty bastard, and Tom Winshaw, amateur balaclava wearer and head boy of Lord Sutton College, are both dead and may God have mercy upon their souls. Well, mercy upon Tom's soul. Brian, as I think I've mentioned before, really had it coming, so I don't much care what happens to his soul.

Summer Vacation
&
Poems

❀

Kamala Nair

I STOOD STILL on the hot clay tennis court and scowled into the sun. It burned on, unsympathetic.

Wanting to stay home and read, I had waited by the window all morning, praying for rain. But not even a single cloud interrupted the sky's blueness. My mother insisted I attend my daily tennis lesson, which had become a dreaded summer ritual.

'I don't want you wasting a beautiful July day indoors,' she said, then buckled me into the backseat and drove me and my willing older sister to the local high school courts.

All around me bored girls swatted at neon tennis balls like flies. Tucking the toe of my sneaker behind the scuffed baseline, I fidgeted with the handle of my racket.

My sister stood on the other side of the net, the clean, rounded lines of her body poised into a graceful arc. She swung with expert precision.

A quick wind knifed the still heat and I felt for a split second the woolly fuzz of a tennis ball against my earlobe.

'Heads up!' yelled Bryce, the tennis coach, running a hand through his sandy hair. 'That,' he said, fixing his eyes on me, 'was a close shave.'

Bryce, captain of the high school tennis team and the thief of my heart. I chased after the ball, pumping my skinny limbs like an awkward windmill. I heard Bryce complimenting my sister on her serve. She was the uncontested star of the class.

I was twelve years old, gawky and exposed in my flat tee-shirt and sticky shorts, ugly as an ungroomed poodle. Humiliated, I sent the ball sailing back over the net.

My sister returned it with a firm volley. I drew my arm back and kept my eye focused on the ball, which spun forward like a comet. Wanting to make up for my blunder, and my skin hot under Bryce's expectant blue gaze, I hit the ball with all my might, only to send it smacking into the top of the net, then bouncing back and rolling toward me in defeat.

'Let's work on your backspin,' smiled Bryce, revealing a row of very white, very straight teeth. Coming around to my side of the net, he stood behind me and placed his tanned, sinewy arms over mine. His closeness alerted my nostrils to the scent of sweat and freshly laundered white cotton. The face of my racket swayed from side to side, making a soft breeze as he swung me back and forth.

'That's it, that's it,' he encouraged.

Blood rushed to my cheeks. The fledgling down on my arms prickled. So this is what it was like. I closed my eyes and allowed myself to be guided through a perfect forehand.

The moment ended quickly. He took a few steps back, then shoved his hands into the deep pockets of his shorts.

'OK, let's call it a day,' he announced, and the class breathed a collective sigh of relief. 'Who wants to help me put away the balls?'

My sister volunteered, and Bryce grinned, looking pleased.

'Why don't you go wait for Mom in the parking lot,' my sister instructed me, and unwanted, I followed the throng of girls through the chain link fence.

Most of the mothers were already waiting, smiling broadly as they stood against their station wagons and offered Gatorade to their sweaty daughters. I looked around for my mother and did not see her. One by one, cars disappeared until the parking lot was empty.

The summer school kids began to file out of the high school for their lunch break. I turned back to the tennis court and saw my sister with her back facing me, strands of her pert ponytail coming loose and sticking through the chain link fence. Bryce was standing close to her, and she was giggling at whatever he was saying. The tennis balls still wandered like aimless satellites around the court. My heart turned over with envy.

I walked onto the grassy lawn that stretched between the school and the parking lot. A striped bee circled my ankle momentarily, then moved onto a more enticing yellow dandelion. I rehearsed the angry words I would spout to my mother for being late.

Then I noticed a small group of boys standing under the shade of a giant maple tree, staring at something. I edged toward their loose circle, curious. One of the boys, who wore his hair in a stringy rat-tail, was holding a bottle of water and pouring it over the grass. Everyone laughed.

As I approached I saw at the center of their cluster a tiny gray bird lying on the ground, its damp feathers flinching with every spurt of cold water that trickled from the tormentor's bottle. I watched them, transfixed, a sour taste curdling on my tongue. Another boy picked up a stick and began to prod the bird.

'Is it dead?' he asked.

'No,' said the other. 'It's still moving.'

I looked over my shoulder at the tennis court. Bryce's arms had migrated from his pockets to the small of my sister's back. I saw that he was kissing her, and that her smooth brown legs were wrapped around his waist like a ribbon.

Confused tears suddenly stinging my eyes, I turned back to the boys. The one with the rat-tail raised his flashy hi-topped sneaker. I realized what he was about to do, and lurched forward involuntarily.

'Don't!' I blurted.

Surprised, the boy faltered and dropped his foot, just missing the bird's neck and leaving a harsh imprint on the grass. They all turned to me with hostile eyes and I returned their glare like a fool.

The class bell rang.

'Freak!' one of them snorted derisively, and they all turned and ran back toward the school.

I kneeled down on the earth and examined the injured bird. I touched a blurry charcoal wing with the tip of my finger, then stroked it. The dark pearl of its eye stared up into the tree. With the edge of my tee-shirt I wiped away the drops of water clumped on its feathers. Its beak opened and closed slightly, a sliver of pink tongue lolled against a blade of grass.

I lifted the bird and cupped it in my hands. Perhaps my mother would let me stay home from tennis lessons to care for the bird. Perhaps this could be my summer project. The bird's softness tickled the skin between my fingers. I felt the pinprick of its heart against my palm.

I thought of the bed I would make for the bird in my room, a small shoebox lined with grass on the window sill. I would start out with a diet of seeds, then when it finally rained, I would nourish the bird back to health with earthworms that scattered like loose strands of thread on our driveway.

An insistent honk interrupted my reverie. My mother's station wagon pulled into the parking lot. She was smiling apologetically and waving at me through the window. A large tree obscured her view of the tennis court. I looked back and saw my sister zipping her racket into its case, her face flushed. Bryce watched her skip away toward the car, his lean cheeks dimpled into a satisfied smile. Then his eyes suddenly shifted and met mine. He saw me staring, mouth agape. I could not look away. He brought his finger to his lips, then winked at me, as if we now shared some intimate secret.

I got up and my legs wobbled. The bird shivered in my fist and I felt it grow heavy like a stone. Bending down again, I let the bird go, back onto its patch of wet grass. The bird's chest puffed up with a tiny breath, a fragile curtain descended over its eye. I crouched over the dying creature and fingered the deep lines the grass had cut into my knees.

My mother pressed the horn again. I knew that Bryce would be dreaming about my pretty sister tonight, that the sun would blaze on for the rest of the summer, and that tomorrow would be another tortuous tennis lesson, just like this one.

My Father's Village

In late summer, when the fuchsia hibiscus
open like bright kisses, and under wet rocks
slim cobras sleep out the afternoon heat,
I come back to your youth.

I come to your old, peeling house
to find you small and bare-faced,
sailing paper boats on a swollen river.

Frogs unfold like green sea flowers
from the plentiful well.
The dusty lawn is plump with life.

I pass through the soggy paddy field,
past the rubber trees sticky with sap,
to the village square where

Your gentle mother buys a dozen mangoes
to feed a dozen hungry beggars.
In the hospital, your father ministers
to the villagers, hysterical with illness.

I come with my crayons, coloring in the lines
you draw for us every night over the dinner table.

I come like a blind woman feeling in the dark,
wresting the angels of memory you worship
from the stiff family portrait

As if I might erase the mad indignity,
the withering moth of old age, as if
I could repaint the brilliance of the house
you remember.

Hunted

I see the falcon, his eye prised
Open bronze and wide as a zero,
Moved by his insatiable hunger
To trounce the fragile nest below.
It is only a matter of time
Before he trounces me also.
Bodies bow like flesh before him,
The pillaged treetops crown him king.
He stalks the night to ease his craving
And rapes the wind with bracken wing.
Up the rocks I clamber to escape
His atrocious, searching glare,
A throttled sunset lights my cave
And tells him I am there.

The Calf

Sweet calf,
I love your proud black spots and
Your dumb black bullfrog eyes.
All day you lie in the green field,
Yellow flowers churning like butter
Under a blue sky, and you
Indulge in the sweetness
Of that green grass.
Letting the false milk seep
Into your second stomach
You forget your mother.
But I remember her at night
When I can't sleep, and I count
The cows filing out of their pens
One by one,
In organized lines, their suctioned udders
Swaying like pink hearts
As they move along the runway
Toward death.

Punting

That day the boats
A flotilla of wooden spoons
Skimmed the waters of the river Cherwell.
Lying with my face upturned
I saw only the cape of unmarred sky
As you moved the wet earth.
To me, we glided pleasantly.
I did not see then how you agitated the water
Cautiously, as if you caressed
The cheek of a leper.

We set sail on the river like it was the sea
And after awhile you let me steer.
I bumped against the banks, the willow above
Sweeping across my face, while you sat
Self-possessed.
I had only a slender spear
To balance us. Looking back, I see
How even the brightness of that day could not stop
The refraction of darkness on the river's prism.

The Next Season

You've stopped writing back. Days pass and I pull
The numbers from my calendar like loose teeth.

Months ago when it was warm, I burned
Like fever on your skin. You've sloughed me off.

I wait, up to my knees in dead leaves. I wring the sheets
Each night, knotting and unknotting my hair

Until the darkness crumbles
Into morning's cruel bruise. In the coldness I picture you:

Angel of indifference, jungle sphinx, smiling
As your copper studs slowly turn my earlobes green.

When it finally begins to snow I will burn your letters.
Their ashes will dance like coal feathers.

I will make a dark scar on the snow,
Scraping through ice with my steel shovel.

Embalmed chin-deep in icy waters, like Tantalus,
Your lips taste their last fruit.

The Suburban Lynx

Sabina Conerney

Tom patted his oily, balding hair and rubbed his hands in glee. He walked briskly out the front gate and closed it confidently behind him. Whistling with victory, he made his way down the deserted street to his black Mercedes, all the time gripping the cheque in his left pocket with a sweaty palm. Yet another fool fiddled, he grinned to himself, settling into the soft leather and fastening the seat belt around his enormous belly. With a roaring of the engine he accelerated, narrowly missing a small dog on the side of the pavement.

Tom was a self-employed door-to-door salesman, lacking in qualifications and a licence to sell, but making up for these penalties with a crafty mind and the art of persuasion. As a young man fresh from completing his Leaving Certificate, he had had aspirations to become a car salesman, but had quit the job two weeks in, following an intense row with his boss. The latter had informed Tom that his appalling attitude meant that no person in their right mind would buy a car from him. Tom took this to be an expression of jealousy at his cleverness and promptly left. The truth was that Tom, while he was exceptionally talented at the promotion of virtually anything under the sun, experienced a shocking transition of temperament when he realised that the customer in question was not going to buy. Early on, Tom had realised that the effect of his imposing presence was halved if he faced more than one customer at the same time. Couples could stand up to him and were likely to report him if he became rude. He also realised that people were less likely to buy if they could walk off the premises, under the guise of coming back later. The trick, Tom discovered, was to target unsuspecting people who were alone in their houses. He had started off with housewives in the 1980s and had been forced to resort to pensioners as the former gradually wised-up to him. Old people had long lost the art of slamming the door before Tom had his foot in it. They had no chance of using the excuse of coming back later, either. They could hardly leave their own homes and Tom had no intention of departing without a sale. They were also the easiest to spot—their gardens were usually overgrown or their front doors badly needed a lick of paint.

Following his departure from car sales, Tom had made the decision to be self-employed. His experience in the company had cemented his hatred of authority and only served to heighten his self-importance. He decided to become a door-to-door salesman, knowing that the best skill he possessed was his craftiness. The problem lay in finding the perfect product to sell. In order to be successful at every house he visited, he would have to offer a ware that the homeowner could not outwardly refuse. It was no good promoting the advantages of new windows or household furniture – the person could easily reply that they did not wish to replace either. As his sole purpose was to cheat the customer, he did not want to become involved in goods that would be closely monitored by consumer regulations. But what, he wondered, could he sell?

Tom took his time in deciding which product to choose. Despite being only nineteen years of age, he had already left home and moved himself into his great-aunt's house. She had welcomed the company and had refused to charge Tom rent. Tom had heard rumours that the old woman, whose immediate family were all dead and who had never married, was likely to be put into a nursing home by relations, due to her increasingly forgetful state. Sure enough, within weeks of his moving in, the elderly lady had moved to a nursing home several miles away. Tom had 'volunteered' to stay and take care of the house. He had thus secured his accommodation and eliminated such expenses. He even withdrew the elderly woman's pension every week for 'household expenses'.

One night, an idea occurred to him as he lay in the bath. As he soaked, reflecting the day and wondering for the umpteenth time how he could make his millions, his eyes fell upon the new bar of soap that he had placed in the dish. He picked it up and began, ever so gently, to run his hands over the logo that was moulded into the soap. Within minutes, he had made it disappear. He sat motionless for a second and suddenly, placing the soap down, he climbed quickly out of the bath and ran down the stairs two at a time. The heavy carpet prevented him from slipping, although he skidded slightly in the hall and broke his fall only by gripping the banisters and knocking over a small vase that lay on a delicate oak table. Tom didn't care about the vase. The fragments of china were incidental to him now as he ran, stark naked, into the kitchen and out into the back garden.

The garden was one of those lovely old leafy havens that are found in the older Dublin suburbs. It was long and sheltered, encased between tall hedges and overrun with colourful flowers that had lived there for years. The heavenly scent of roses hung deliciously on the night air and mingled with the honeysuckle that had entwined itself around the door. Tom, who had been oblivious to its beauty before, now saw it in an entirely new light. *Flowers.* Everywhere he looked there were flowers. He let out a sudden, manic laugh and began tearing around the garden. Why hadn't he seen it before? It was brilliant! It was ingenious! Look at the colours of them! Look at the abundance of them! With one swift action, he tore a rose viciously from a bush and laughed again. He began dancing on the spot until, without warning, a thorn embedded itself deeply into his upper thigh. He kicked the base of the bush with venom, cursing profusely and decided to retreat indoors. Within seconds he was back in the bathroom, rotating his finger once more around the bar of soap, which had set slightly in his absence. With the addition of a little water, it became soft once more. Tom now shredded the rose petals into the sink and proceeded to place them, ever so delicately, onto the soap. They stuck with ease to the lather. He left the soap sitting in a dish on the windowsill, cleaned off his feet in the now lukewarm bath water and dried himself, whistling a little tune as he did so. With one last look at his brainchild, he headed off to bed.

The following morning, as soon as his eyelid had revealed the dawning of a new day, Tom had leapt out of bed and into the bathroom. The soap lay in the dish and, just as he had planned, the rose particles were solidly attached. Tom eased it out of the dish and looked at it in wonder. It looked exactly like the expensive soap convalescents often received in hospital. He brought it up to his nose. The delicious aroma of roses enveloped his nostrils. He let out a whoop and began dancing a bizarre little jig on the bathroom tiles. The house rocked slightly under his weight. Despite being a young man just out of his teens, Tom's pot belly was already in full development. Following a hurried breakfast fry, he jumped into his car and drove directly to a haberdashery in the city, where he purchased a large quantity of gauzy scraps of material that were on sale, as well as a roll of shiny pink ribbon. On his way home, he popped into the local chemist and picked up a collection of cheap soaps that were on special offer. By that evening, a mini business had come alive in Tom's great-aunt's bathroom and several flowers in the back garden were without their heads. Tom stood amongst the soaps, frothing at the mouth at the thought of the money that he would make from his idea. He was careful to make sure that the logos on the soaps were fully melted off as he added various petals to them. As they dried, he covered them in fussy pieces of gauze and tied them elegantly with ribbon.

By night time, Tom had twenty-five expensive-looking soaps at his disposal. By the following evening, he had sold the lot. Many customers were interested in the 'organic' soaps that were made from 'natural ingredients'. They had let Tom in the door and had listened in awe as he explained how his product guaranteed softer skin, promoted well-being and was the only soap of its kind in Ireland. They failed to notice how he cut across them when they attempted to ask after the price. Tom had a knack of knowing when a customer was about to request this. He could skilfully read the drop in the tone of their voice. Irish customers were so deliciously polite. Within minutes, many of them were reaching for their purses and it was only after they realised that their chequebook was needed that they discovered they had been too hasty. But by then, it was too late and Tom's hand was already offering them the use of his ballpoint pen.

As the years wore on, the ballpoint pen that Tom had initially used became a gleaming, gold-plated one and the cloth on his back became more expensive. He began dining out at the fanciest restaurants and drinking in hotels as opposed to his local public house. It was in one of these hotels that he met his wife, a woman who shared a similar outlook on life to himself and whose beady eyes had taken in his lavish lifestyle. Within two years they had married, neither really caring for the other. Tom had wanted a good-looking wife; she had wanted a wealthy husband. The two had agreed not to have children as Tom was worried that they would burn a hole in his pocket and his wife was worried about stretchmarks. However, as the years went by, Tom began to appreciate her companionship. As long as she had money, she didn't complain. She was a peaceful woman to live with and he missed her when she wasn't there. In fact, he found himself worrying if she became delayed in town and heaving a sigh of relief when he heard her stilettos on the pavement.

Now, as Tom roared off down the road in his beautiful car, his eyes caught sight of a young woman shaking her fist at him and picking up the small dog he had almost run over. He shoved his middle finger up behind the glass and sped off. Tom was getting sick of the growing confidence of the Irish population. Old people were actually asking him to declare himself through speakers installed beside their front doors. Many pulled back the net curtains of their windows and looked at him, quickly retreating back into the safety of their homes. Tom usually retaliated with a gob of spit onto their driveway and walked off, nearly taking the hinges off their gate with force as he left. How dare they be so insolent! How dare they insult him! If there was one thing Tom detested, it was a cheeky pensioner. He hated their suspicious looks through the window, their shrivelled fingers confidently gripping their panic alarms. Tom liked to be feared. He liked to dazzle the customer with his sharp suit and his bleached smile. From the beginning of his business he had searched for a suitable nickname for himself, something befitting his craftiness. Rommel had been the Desert Fox. That was a good, powerful title. Could he modify it in any way? Finally, having thumbed through a book on animals from the library that, incidentally, he did not return, Tom had decided to call himself the Suburban Lynx. The only problem was that the Suburban Lynx seemed to have lost his knack for victims. They were trying to outwit him and nobody, absolutely nobody, was allowed to out-wit Tom.

As he headed towards town, musing over the good old days, Tom began to worry. Business had been dropping steadily since the nineties. He had become increasingly aware of his wife's spending habits. She would have to cut down until they were back on track. He frowned as he noticed yet another crack in his leather seat. He had started the day in a good mood as he had devised a new way to trick customers into opening their doors. Following a knock on the door of a house that, due to the filth of its windows, had to belong to someone elderly, he had bent down to tie his shoelace. He could sense the old person looking out, wondering if the man bent forward on their driveway was someone they knew. Within minutes the door had been opened, Tom's large frame had been exposed and a cheque had been written. However, as he looked at the young woman in his rear view mirror, he knew that he had been lucky. That old person would not be fooled again. Tom was also growing sick and tired of waiting while old people made their way laboriously to answer the door. In his youth he had been pre-pared to wait, but now he was becoming increasingly impatient and, he hated to admit, too old to stand for long periods of time. Tom was forty-four now and had not aged well. His high-living had rendered him overweight, he had more skin on his head than hair and his hands were continuously dry from constantly handling soap.

The truth was, Tom was slowing down and, while he had retained his youthful arrogance, the confidence of the noughties consumer was diminishing his resolve. People were becoming too bloody self-assured. Only the other day he had knocked at the door of a house whose lawn looked like it hadn't been cut in several years. Instead of an old person answering, however, Tom had found himself face-to-face with a crowd of hungry students, naked from the waist up, who were expecting a pizza delivery. They had actually laughed at him! Laughed at his wares and told him that, as they never washed, they wouldn't be purchasing a gram of his soap. Tom didn't dare to be rude to them. It wasn't worth the risk. However, as he made his way in humiliation out of the front gate, he put out his foot and tripped-up the pizza delivery man on his way in. Let someone else be the centre of embarrassment − it certainly wasn't going to be him. As he steered round a corner, Tom reminded himself that he was not going to give up. For several years now he had attempted to sell his 'home-made' soap to chemists around the country. The thing was, many chemists were not prepared to buy from Tom because he charged too much money. They argued that nobody would pay such outrageous prices.

The only chemist that bought from Tom was O' Hara's, the reason for this being that the proprietor of the business was a school friend of Tom's. Seamus had known Tom since secondary school and had been intimidated into giving the latter his homework for the six years of their second level education. Seamus was a shy man who had never married. He had recently inherited the family business and was determined to make a go of it. Tom had seen the opportunity immediately and had informed Seamus that he would supply him with soap every fortnight for a reasonable price. Tom's 'reasonable' price was actually higher than he charged other chemists.

He had no conscience about this—Seamus was a well-off man who, Tom believed, should be more than happy to do him a favour. Every two weeks, he arrived with more soap, noticing how Seamus had been forced to sell it at 70% less than the cost price. Contrary to feeling guilty, Tom's disrespect for Seamus only increased.

Tom steered slowly into his estate, deep in thought. He would be alright. He *never* lost. He absentmindedly reached out of the car window, tearing the heads from two lone daffodils that stood on a patch of grass by the pavement. Tom never missed an opportunity to collect petals for his soaps. He drove around at night, ripping the heads from as many flowers as he could find. Indeed, he had been doing this for so long that it was considered a local phenomenon. Many people had resigned themselves to having a bare lawn and had concentrated on cutting their hedges into fancy patterns instead. Some had even purchased fake flowers and had arranged them delicately in large terracotta pots by their front doors.

He forced himself to whistle as he pulled into the driveway. Business might be down, he mused, but Seamus was the key to his future success. He could increase his order of soap or, Tom jingled the door keys, maybe stupid old Seamus would be interested in a business partnership? Fitting the key into the lock, he opened the door, only to find a solicitor's letter on the hall table. His wife had, as usual, opened his mail. Clutching the letter in horror, he realised with shock that several soap manufacturers were suing him for altering and illegally selling their product. There was no way out of this—the game was up. He ran to the window in a frenzy and looked out, suddenly paranoid that he was being watched. The bare lawns seemed to close in on him as he looked up and down the street. It was like Winter out there—cold-hearted and depressing—and he wrenched the curtains closed to get away from it.

Trembling with anger and panic, he made his way up the stairs and into his room. His wife lay on the bed, dressed in the silk lingerie he had bought her that Christmas. All at once he felt a sharp pain in his stomach and a surge of vomit poisoned his oesophagus as Seamus, bony and pasty-white, emerged naked from the en suite.

Two Chapters

(extract from a novel)

Geraldine McMenamin

CHAPTER 1

THE SUMMER HOUSE is a strange name for one of the most unusual buildings I know. It is located in the wooded part of the estate, on a cliff that overhangs a small river.

She had it built in the seventies at a time when she was at her most admired; a society dame with enough money to spend on an expensive post-modern architect. Few people in the country would have used architects in those days. But not her, she had to have the very best of everything.

Michael Wright had indeed achieved a classic when he chose steel and glass to house what became the most important room on the estate. Enormous steel girders had to be transported, in sections, through the forest, and then welded together before they were secured into the river bed. These enormous girders rose sixty feet up the cliff edge and formed the foundations. Each of the four walls in the rectangular-shaped building was made of flawlessly clear glass that extended from floor to ceiling. The structure started at the end of the forest path and extended through the trees and over the river. It had cost a small fortune to build. 'A scandalous waste', I had heard one of the gardeners say.

To some, when it was first built, it must have seemed odd to use such harsh materials with the gentler surroundings of the wild oak forest and the river bed. It was a stark contrast, a bold statement of how she could dominate everything and everyone around her.

Somehow, I imagined that would have pleased her. That's how she would have liked to have been perceived: a hard bitch in a soft world.

Things don't always work out as planned, however, and with time the summer house had blended in too well with its surroundings. The trees had grown taller and obscured the view from the inside so that in many ways it felt like an enclosed tree house. Shrubs on the river bank had wildly wound their way up the cliff edge and were now encroaching on the house corners. Moss had lodged itself successfully on the flat roof. Vines of flowering clematis and vigorous Virginia creeper had engaged with the steel girders as if they were trying to drag the structure back into the forest floor.

No attempt was made to stop this onslaught and I always felt that nature would win out in the end. I imagined some future archaeologist or alien being discovering the summer house and concluding that the forest had come alive to gobble up the invader.

It was, without doubt, my favourite place. When I came back to the estate that long-ago summer, she had more or less abandoned it. Its style of architecture had gone out of vogue and it had been built before the concept of insulation had been perfected. It was cold.

She had built a replica Victorian conservatory onto the main house, and that's where she had now held her evening soirées.

'The path to the summer house is so charming but it absolutely ruins one's heels,' I had overheard her say to one of her many visitors.

That suited me just fine. I had practically lived there that summer long ago when I was forced to come and stay with her. After a long tramp around the estate in the mornings, I would spend the day in there painting and listening to the Stones and David Bowie.

I met some local lads from the village and sometimes a gang of them would come along with their girlfriends and sisters and friends and we would all hang out there. I showed them a way to break into the estate so that they didn't have to go past the main house.

In the evenings, if she wasn't around, I would have soirées of my own with stolen beer and home-grown weed. No one knew what went on there, or at least if they did, I wasn't made aware of it. I was left alone in the summer house, using it as my refuge, my only solace, my sanity.

Now, it feels strange to be back on the estate again, and even stranger to find that she is not in the main house. She is not languishing in the grand drawing room, ordering her assistants about, or being rude and intimidating on the phone to one of her many suppliers or staff.

When I call to the main house, Charlie tells me that she has all but moved into the summer house. She has shunned the luxuries of her own bedroom suite and has insisted in being transported down to the summer house in a wheelchair. Her bed has been moved along with her toiletries, as well as all the medication and any clothes that she needs.

'It's too cold, Charlie. That cold summer house can't be good for her.'

'Oh no, it's all been renovated now,' he tells me. I inhale sharply at the thought of what she has done to *my* summer house.

Charlie gives me all this news in his soft Kerry voice over a cup of tea in the kitchen. I have never understood why he has stayed with her for so long. He is handsome, in his own way, and reliable and capable of any task she ever gives him. He could have worked for anyone. He could have had a family of his own. He could have gone away to America like his brothers. But no, some part of him has remained loyal to her above everything else, and he is still here making arrangements for her till the very end.

He is a shy man and it took me by surprise when I received his call two days ago.

'She doesn't know I am calling you, you understand, don't you Miss? It's just that… well… I know her, I know her right well and I know she'd like to see you.'

Instinctively, I knew that I had to make this journey to see her one more time. I hastily made arrangements with my ex-partner to mind our son and left my hectic life in Dublin to come here, to the kitchen to have my cup of tea with Charlie and try to be sad.

In a way, I am angry that she has any power at all over me. I have to keep reminding myself that she hasn't asked me to come. 'Would she do the same for me?' I ask myself again and again. I don't think so.

Charlie said she would be waking up soon from her afternoon nap and it would be a good time to see her. Now I find myself reluctantly walking back down the forest path. It is such a long time since I have been here that I can barely find my way. I am watching out for the original garish structure at the end of the track, and when I don't see it, immediately I think I have taken a wrong turn. I retrace my steps and start again and this time I know I am right. Just as I reach the end of the path I catch a glimpse of some reflected light. 'My God, it's one of the windows,' I think to myself. The summer house is now almost completely obscured by growth. What started years ago continued unchecked. I am confused. What did Charlie mean when he said it was renovated?

At least the sliding entrance door is in the same place but now it moves silently when I open it. It is no longer cold inside. She must have installed heating.

The light is temporarily fading outside as an overcast cloud passes and it takes a moment or two for my eyes to adjust to the darkness inside. I can see her big old iron bed facing the valley window. I walk quietly towards it, afraid to disturb her sleep. I stop a few feet away from the bed, suddenly fearful again, as I have always been with her. I notice the sound of her breath, and its slow uneasy rattling becomes the loudest sound on earth. I am about to turn tail and run when slowly she opens her eyes and smiles at me. I stand in shock and cannot recognise this new look.

'Darling, am I dreaming or are you really here?' she asks in a low voice.

'No, you're not dreaming. It's me, Mother. It's me.'

CHAPTER 2

THAT NIGHT CHARLIE lets me pick any room I want in the main house.

'I stay at the mews house now in what used to be the old stable yard, you remember that, don't you, a stór?'

'Yes, yes, of course I remember it.' But in truth my memory is very hazy, clouded over like the misty forest that surrounds this big house.

He senses my unease. 'It's all done up now. It's a lovely job. You can have a good look round in the morning and I'm sure you'll remember it better.'

Yes, in the morning everything will seem clearer, I tell myself.

Charlie insists on making me a sandwich in what is the only familiar room in the main house. The kitchen remains unchanged with the big old pine table and chairs, willow patterned china on the dresser and the copper pans hanging above the Aga. The cooker is not lit, though, and somehow the soul of the room is missing.

He chit-chats about the house and the staff and the estate. Details that are not important, not now. I am detached. This is his world, she is its centre. I am apart.

Charlie pours me out a cup of tea from a big brown earthenware pot and plonks a large glass of Irish whiskey beside it. At first I decline but, as I know he will, he insists and eventually I accept.

He bids me goodnight and tells me to feel free to look around the house.

I climb the stairs from the basement and wander from room to room, whiskey in hand. It is beginning to taste warmer, better, like I need some more. I find a cut glass decanter half full in the formal dining room and help myself.

I find it curious that for so many years I carried a picture of this house around in my head and that picture had no clear focus; the camera was at the wrong setting. Whereas everything here used to be posh and expensive and unattainable, I now only see its charm and taste and beauty. The William Morris wallpaper, the velvet drapes, the handmade Donegal carpet, the Irish silver, the Derek Hill print. Everything is perfectly placed, put in position a long time ago, and still the same.

On I wander, across the wide hall with the evening sun squinting through the fanlight over the wide Georgian door. Through to the drawing room with the Parker Knoll couches and the Country Life magazines neatly stacked on the coffee table. I feel as if I am in a museum, viewing her life through the series of silver framed photos on the mantelpiece. Curious then that she has none of her childhood, as if she only came to life when she married Edgar. Of course she has none of me or my Jack. I would expect that. Even so, it still hurts.

I find myself in her study, fingering the leather-topped desk, eyeing the wall-to-wall books on the shelves. It is the end of May and the evening light is finally fading, so I turn on a light to continue my casual inspection.

The addition of electricity makes me feel like an intruder now, guilty that I have invaded her private space, nervous that Charlie will think that I am snooping.

I am not ready to see the framed painting above the fireplace. At first I cannot understand why it is familiar, certainly not a famous artist, a vibrant oil with strong colours of a woodland, almost abstract. Then the startling truth hits: it's mine. Yes, for sure it's one of the paintings I did that summer messing about around the estate. I wonder why she kept it. I didn't think she even knew I had painted that summer. How strange that she should frame it and keep it here, of all places, her private study; a place I felt was always out of bounds. Am I completely wrong about her?

I decide to stop searching for things I do not understand and leave the study, in case I find something else. I am exhausted. I grab my bag from the hall and decide it's time for sleep. I pick the pink room, the one with roses on the wallpaper and a matching bed cover. The whiskey has made me light-headed and it is as much as I can do to brush my teeth and flop into bed.

The bed is higher than I am used to, and the pillows harder. Despite these unfamiliar surroundings I fall into a deep, deep sleep.

I dream that I am sleeping with my Jack when he was a toddler. His soft curly hair is long and uncut. His cheeks are rosy red from teething. His pyjamas have Barbar the Elephant on them and are all soft and fleecy. His chubby face rests between my neck and right shoulder. He is asleep but I am not. I am awake and drinking in the warmth of his little body, his perfect form. I am in that tranquil place between love and peace. I am full.

Then the dream changes and Jack is on the forest path to the summer house. He hasn't got enough clothes on and I am worried he will be cold.

He keeps running ahead of me and hiding behind the bushes. I am nervous. I don't like this game. I can't see him enough. I keep calling him and calling him but he doesn't reappear. Something seems to be holding me back. I can't keep up with him. He is going further and further away. I am screaming for him now and crying. I lose sight of him completely. I begin to panic. Where is he? What should I do? Should I fetch Charlie? No, no I must go on and keep looking and keep calling. I can't waste time going back to the main house.

'Jack, Jack, where are you? Mummy's got some chocolate for you, just come out and you can have some chocolate.'

I am running now down the forest path, completely panicked. Suddenly, I see him. He's crawling on the forest floor, but no, that's not right, he's crawling on something higher. Dear God, it's the summer house roof. He's on the roof and he's going to fall all the way down to the river bed.

Sixty feet at least! I can't stop him. I clamber up the house and try to coax him to me. He keeps crawling further towards the edge. Something holds me back. I can't get him. What's holding me? Why can't I move?

I turn and see *her* hand on my ankle. She has come out of the summer house in her nightclothes. She's all thin and frail like she was in the bed but now she's strong too. She won't let go.

'Let him go child, let him go,' she says as I start screaming. I can't shake her off.

Suddenly, I am aware that I am dreaming. I toss and turn with violence and force myself awake. I sit up with a start and find the room is bathed in morning light. I am wet with sweat and shaking. My mouth is dry from the whiskey and I need some water.

Unsteady and unhappy, I make my way downstairs. It's only 6 a.m. by the grandfather clock in the hall. It's too early to ring Karl and see if Jack's alright.

It's only a dream, it's only a dream, I keep telling myself. I pour out a big glass of cold water, drink, and refill it.

I am on my way back upstairs when I hear the phone ring. It takes me a while to find it. It's coming from her study. I pick it up.

'Hello, look I'm awfully sorry for ringing so early, but could I speak to Helen Fitzgerald, please?' says Karl on the other end.

'Karl, it's me. What's the matter?' I ask.

In a strange way I know what's coming. I know from the tone of his voice.

'Helen, it's Jack. Jack's gone missing.'

My knees soften and slowly I fall to the floor.

No News, No Shoes

੪੪

James Sumner

I HAVE A PICTURE of myself at London Heathrow wearing rose-tinted national health glasses, a new romantic haircut and a pink Hawaiian shirt. I took a vow not to arrive back from holiday looking like a twat. However, years later, I was pushing a trolley through customs at 06.20 on a Tuesday morning in January at Heathrow, dressed in black shorts, a Billabong short-sleeved shirt and no shoes.

I had taken Victoria, my wife, to Omanalak in the Maldives. It was a nothing-to-do-and-all-day-to-do-it type of place. The island had rabbits that slinked around, twitching their noses like uptight guests. I hate airports, catching planes and British Airways, but not in that order. On the outward leg, after 24 hours of hot and cold towels, I clocked the other whiteys waiting for the yellow-and-blue seaplane but avoided any eye contact. We were met on a pontoon slung over floating barrels and a hand-carved sign saying *Omanalak International Airport*. We transferred, jet-lagged and in silence. I smelt so bad that I could smell myself. A speedboat took us to the island. It was impossible to see the villas from the boat, such was the detail paid to the design of the accommodation. Before we arrived, we were given a shoe bag with *No News, No Shoes*.

The smaller the place you stay in, the more people you meet but I was not fussed whether I met anybody or not. Having unpacked our suitcases, I busied myself putting the other guests into little boxes.

73

It is human nature to mull over the scant information about the bodies promenading up and down. There was a strict caste system based on how many times you had visited before. Guests who had stayed there before were keen to show their social credentials:

—Are you from England?

—London.

—Oh.

—St John's Wood. Yeh, big house there. Place in Barbados too.

—Nice. Is it you travelling with the two sons?

—Archie, now reading Classics, is up at Oxford and Charlie, who's brighter than his brother, last year at Harrow. You're from Ireland?

—Yes.

—I went to a reception at the Guinnesses. Do you know the Guinnesses?

—No.

—Oh.

I wanted to say that I didn't know anyone but she had turned round to help herself to fruit from Ahmed, the Fruit Man. You had to admire the skill and dexterity of the gentlemanly Fruit Man. The Fruit Man had brought from Sri Lanka a fantastic smile and a set of gnashers that Americans would die for. He would select, wash, slice and peel exotic fruits for breakfast every morning. There was a causal relationship between time spent watching The Fruit Man and time spent sitting in the can. We also got pally with Mr. Choppy Choppy, who could cook the world from his own wok. I warned him not to take his wok home. As a first year *arriviste*, I had more in common with the waiters than the guests, who were moist with self-love; the type who sported sunglasses as a hair accessory in mid-winter.

One day morphed into another. We'd get up, discuss how we got bitten by mozzies only when we slept under a mosquito net, go to breakfast, eat too much fruit and rush back to the room to defecate anything up to 65% of our total body weight. By about 10.30, I was absolutely Hank Marvin and had to wait till lunch. Then we would argue whether to go snorkelling before or after lunch and therefore whether to sunbathe pre-or-post lunch. Lunch, then spa, read, sun downer, mozzie spray, then supper and bed. I didn't know what day it was and it didn't matter.

Christmas Eve was overcast but still hot enough for me to look like a beetroot. The entertainment was provided by the flying fish throwing themselves on the beach so that the guests could throw them back into the water. At night, there was a cocktail reception with free champagne held on a blinding white spit of sand, followed by the showpiece Christmas Eve buffet. Guests were clambering around, videoing the buffet, which took them between 10 and 15 minutes. By the time I had walked around the buffet and heard the chefs answer the question, 'What's that?' in every language, I was stuffed. The fare was to be photographed rather than ploughed into.

Christmas Day was like every other day, except that we had a Buck's Fizz before a dip in the Indian Ocean, served between 32-33 degrees; that is to say the ocean, not the drink. I gave my wife a book called *Playing the Moldovans at Tennis* by Tony Hawks, and she gave me a stunning postmodernist tract called *Shit Ground, No Fans*.

On Boxing Day, we woke up and noticed that the high tide had washed away about 20% of our private beach. I thought it was because of the full moon. I was breakfasting with my wife when a wave came up and flooded the dining area on the beach. I thought this was tremendously funny. Everybody started hopping about, all soaking wet. The water did not recoil back to the sea but contin-ued to rise. It was as if somebody had opened a fish tank door. The water did not come up in a battering wave; it rose like water in a canal lock. Guests were walking away from the breakfast area in water up to their ankles. One of the guests, determined to finish his cooked breakfast, was only one rasher away when the first wave came and flooded the table.

We were back at our room when the second wave arrived. My wife was outside the villa; I was inside. The water loomed towards the room, catching the two of us on different sides of the same door handle. When the water came towards my wife, it brought the wooden beach furniture, knocking her over. With the pressure of the water pushing against the villa, I could not push the door open and my wife could not pull the door towards her. We didn't scream for help. Besides, it was only water, for Chrissake, and we are both strong swimmers. After the second wave, the water was up to our knees.

The staff came around and told us to go to the staff quarters. Most of the guests did not listen as they were too busy videoing. The staff quarters were on the highest point of the island, which was 3½ metres above sea level. The flotsam and jetsam from the undergrowth got up to join us in making our way to the staff quarters. Tables, sun-loungers and rusty bikes queued behind us, trying to overtake the guests who were wading up to their waists. Some techno-trance Italians, in skinny tops sprouting spankable faces, coped with their life-threatening condition by moving around the staff quarters to get some rays. They had a huge beach towel which they laid on the ground to prevent people from blocking their sun. I insisted on walking upon it and apologising simultaneously. A French lady, who wore her shorts on her hips to look sexy and who only spoke to her kids while shouting from a distance so that everyone could hear, was talking to the woman with the implausibly large tits from Silicon Valley, who accompanied a balding, paunchy Italian fella. She looked like she was taking her wallet for a walk. I would insist on being in the same lifeboat with them, if only for ballast. A South African family had been rescued by one of the hotel's boats. He was telling us how the water had come up to his chin and how his son had been holding onto a single branch. I told the little boy what a brave boy he was. The little boy turned towards his dad, buried his face and wept.

People became more chatty, offering each other ciggies and sharing bottles of water. One lady said that she'd had a dream at 3.30 a.m. that same morning about a tsunami. I asked her if she could remember what level the Dow Jones would close at. Some guests were indignant that Jeremy, the Manager, had not told them about the tsunami. He told me the only warning he received was from his cat, who had refused to come downstairs the day before the wave came. The guests wanted guarantees. A phone line would have been a start.

By this time, if you could speak the language, it did not matter what school or university you had attended. It was blazing hot, the island paths were less idyllic and now more likely to smell of sewage and were strewn with shoes, clothes, glass and lumps of wooden beach furniture. Technology proved, as always, to be a waste of time. Latest scores coming in: Nature United 1, Technology 0. Tsunami Town 1, Warnings 0.

The General Manager addressed the guests while standing on a table.

—Ladies and Gentleman, as most of you already know, my name is Jeremy Westlake, the General Manager here at Omanalak, and I'd like your attention for a few minutes. We have had an earthquake measuring 8.9 on the Richter scale and a tsunami that arrived at about 10.30 this morning. We had no warning. The Maldives have never had a tsunami before and we've never experienced anything like this. We don't know what will happen, but we must assume more aftershocks will be on their way. We are hearing rumours of typhoons in the Indian Ocean off Sri Lanka, but these are un-confirmed reports. All the lines are down, but as soon as we know any more we will brief you. Meanwhile, could you please collect your valuables from your rooms and reassemble back here. Please wear shoes at all times because of the glass and we'll brief you again with an update at 6 p.m. this evening. Any questions?

—Why didn't we get a warning?

—I have no idea.

—Is there going to be another tsunami?

—I am sorry, I don't know.

—When are the phones going to be up and running?

—We are working on that at the moment.

—How can we evacuate the island if the seaplanes have been smashed to pieces?

—Again, we do not know the particular circumstances of the seaplanes.

—Will you brief us on an hourly basis?

—I would rather brief you when I have information.

—Has anyone seen the rabbits since the wave landed?

—No, I'm afraid not.

A member of staff was ticking our names off the register to see whether people were alive or dead. Thankfully, everybody had been accounted for, which was an enormous relief. A well-known film director, who had blanked everybody the previous week, was finding that people could blank him, too. I tried to rustle up a party to loot the wine cellar and lobbied the sommelier. I offered any member of staff $25 in cash for the first person to confirm the loss of my bill. Guests had to share villas with other guests because of the trashed rooms; a result of the third wave. I told my new friends, Etienne and Valerie, to mind themselves, as the English couple who had offered to put them up were notorious swingers. Our room was smashed to pieces downstairs. The doors had been ripped off and glass was everywhere. Omanalak Resort did not resemble the website or the brochure. The palm trees were lying horizontal. We were lucky the tsunami happened in the morning when people were awake and could see. What would have happened if it had been at night, when everyone was asleep? How can you have a whopping great mobile phone transmitter on the adjacent island, yet nobody can make contact with the outside world?

Having collected the valuables from our room, I put my shoes on and we reconvened in the staff quarters. Worst earthquake in forty years, measuring 9.0 on the Richter scale. Having had the worst earthquake in forty years, did that make it more likely, or less likely, that we would have another one? Were we going to have after-shocks? Were the three waves the warm-up act or the *grand finale?*

By the evening, we had B.B.C News 24 showing us pictures of the destruction in Sri Lanka, Thailand, Indonesia and the Andaman Islands. Nobody had been able to contact the Maldives. My family and friends would be going witless with worry. My son would not know whether his Daddy was alive. I could not believe what I was seeing. My family would be going mad with worry and there was nothing I could do, which made me feel guilty. Having screwed up their Christmas Day by going away, I had reduced them to trembling idiots by Boxing Day, worrying whether I was alive or dead. But there was nothing I could do to alleviate the situation.

An American lady, who called every member of staff by Christian name but who insisted on swatting away guests with her long fingers as if she had snot on her hand, turned around to me while she was watching the TV and said:

—Yeah, funny isn't it?

She turned back towards the TV.

—Fuck off.

I was not about to allow a stranger to suggest that I was laughing at the TV that she was watching and that I had my back to. This was the same guest who insisted the General Manager brief the guests on a hourly basis. She demanded that he evacuate her and her family as a priority. A few days later he told me that she was so rude to his staff that he told her:

—See that boat?

—Yes.

—Well, get on it.

—But I...

—Madam, if you don't get on that boat then you leave me no option but to put you on.

She got on the boat. She had been screaming at the staff because the kids could not watch their DVDs because of the intermittent power supply. The Italian techno-trance trash blamed the Manager for ruining their holiday, and demanded he organise their departure. This he was happy to organise, along with delivering fresh water and tuna to the two neighbouring islands that had been decimated, leaving the inhabitants without electricity, clothing, shelter, food or drink. The Italians left without making a contribution to the Tsunami Fund at Reception, according to my *source*. Neither had the celebrity film director.

—How could anybody possibly know whether the Italians made a donation? asked my wife.

—Who gives a fuck, just make sure we sling them some money, said I.

I did not want to piss anybody off, as I had already lost my cool with Ahmed, the Fruit Man:

—Hi, Ahmed.

—Hello, Mr. Sumner. How can I help?

—I have to make a phone call home. Now.

—All our phones are down at the moment.

—Yeah, I know. But someone must have a phone somewhere. I'll pay. But I must call now, it's an emergency.

—I am very sorry but...

—Look, listen to me: I have to use the fucking phone. I have to ring or fax or text home. I have to. My whole family will be watching this on TV, my Mum and Dad need to know that I'm okay.

—I understand, Sir, but we have no means of communicating with the outside world. None at all.

—Look, I have a son who will be thinking that his Daddy might be dead. Understand?

—Mr. Sumner, my family also on an island. I, too, am unable to know if they are okay.

—I need to ring home like yesterday. Got me?

—Yes, Mr. Sumner, I will do my best. That is my promise.

The next day I would say:

—Hi, Ahmed.

—Hello, Mr. Sumner.

—Any joy with contacting your family yet?

—Not yet, said Ahmed, flashing his patrician smile.

The next day, having finally been able to contact my tearful family, I asked again:

—Hi, Ahmed.

—Good Morning, Mr. Sumner. How are you today?

—Yeah, good thanks. Any news yet?

—No, Mr. Sumner, not yet.

—I'm sure they're fine. I wouldn't even worry, they'll be fine.

Every time, I felt more inept and wished I had never asked. I wanted to let him know that I cared about him but it looked as if I was trying to torment him. I had lost my temper and spoken to him like a spoilt child. And all this 'they'll be fine' malarkey to a bloke for whom knife-wielding was an occupation. The irony of smiling Muslims looking after sour-faced Christians, many of whom were inconsolable at the prospect of facing the New Year without a personal plunge pool, was never far from my mind.

On departure, I said goodbye to all the staff who had congregated down by the pontoon where I had witnessed the first wave. I said goodbye to Ahmed last of all:

—Cheers, big man. Any news?

—Yes, thank you. A member of staff from the hotel has made contact with them. They are all fine, including my son. Thank you. And thank you for asking, Mr. Sumner.

—There were a few days I wished I hadn't...

Ahmed looked at his feet.

—And for Chrissake, Ahmed, will you buy yourself some sharper knives?

Ahmed laughed.

—I'm sorry for going mad at you the other day. You know, about ringing home...

Sorry.

—Please, Mr. Sumner...

—Ahmed, if there is anything, seriously anything that I can do...

—Anything?

Ahmed looked down at my favourite black Oakley sandals.

—For the survivors?

—For the survivors...

I hugged Ahmed good bye. He was waving my favourite black sandals at me when the seaplane took off. After all, it was only a pair of shoes and I could always get another pair of those.

Poems from
'Breakfast with Sylvia'

(Lagan Press 2005)

Kevin Kiely

The Uncrucified Buddha

He squats all gold
unpierced by nails—
head crowned by sunlight
no blood stains, no spear or vinegar
hand raised, the scent of rosewater

you must sit
like a withered tree before a cliff
and be absolutely quiet in concentration

the fragile flesh is sheer gold
tingling with diamonds
the seed-blossoms of the body
float upwards into empty space

inside-outside are equally lit
the eyes begin to blaze
and everything brightens
as if you were in a cloud and felt no gravity

the golden flower is crystallized

and desires cause freefall
as you go through delusions undestroyed
and contemplate the emptiness at the centre
being empty is the strongest delusion

Breakfast with Sylvia Plath

I.

in Café Insomnia, anaemic sunlight
traffic outside
the rain flecked picture window
sizzling bacon, eggs wide eyed
frying on the gas

the face by turns, almond pale and fire bright
a streak of lip paint on the brilliant teeth
she eyes the menu in a seething force-nine rage
her conversation post modern in its tangled sense

bad dreams about a hare
run over by a Morris estate wagon
driven by Edward Hughes
his Meinkampf look (his cock runneth over)
the car with a split screen
two steering wheels, one for her father, Otto
who skinned a rat in front of his students
cooked, and ate it

I won't mention that awful weevil of a woman
I will never speak to God again

Edward Hughes should have
scratched on my tombstone:
it was a fight to the death
she or I
had to die
something of me died with her.

2.
Sivvy ordered
from the tightly clenched menu
pointing with a bandaged thumb

two glasses of milk and bread
nothing else, thank you
the waitress moved off

other tables were served hot food
but the bee keeper's daughter
shrill in convulsive chatter
shaken through the air
crackling with blue light
her bones almost wrenched from the muscles
as if, at any moment the jelly would spill out

fingered a piece of bread,
but did not eat, her milk untouched
then another mood swing:
I lost an overcoat and keys
but I had a spare set—
I sucked but not for long
the sweet and sickly atmosphere
of 23 Fitzroy Road, London NW1

on the wall
outside the front door
a blue plaque to W. B. Yeats
which I knew
was mine too
when I became Christ and Keats

place a dozen yellow roses
in the empty oven, door open
towel inside for a pillow

O my children

Shakespeare & Co

George rules from his riverside bookshop
four storeys high along rue de la Bûcherie
Proudly claiming Walt Whitman as his ancestor—
Shelf after laden-shelf rising like wine racks in the city
The roving eye can soft focus anywhere—a Faber translation
of Laments by Jan Kochanowski

for free accommodation upstairs—you must read a book a day
tend the shop now and then, live on pancakes
chocolate croissants or whatever your budget will allow—
two Londoners outside the kitchen on clarinet and fiddle
play Jazz suite No 2 (Shostakovich)

George seems oblivious among the backpacked youth at table
facing a cracked plate
a fork with sugar on the prongs and a pot of honey (miel)
as he plans another week's rota
for this Shangri-la
where the living and the dead
confront each other

Yesterday she read Coleridge to me

In the car after communion over the phone
Speeding between flood river, tar road and
Tracts of trees honeyed in morning light,
Fast rewind to repeat the music on cassette,
Along the narrow hill-road to Luttrell castle
A pheasant scrambles up a ditch—a shock
Of colour like the rainbow I cling to
And further on, a tangle of sticks in sunglow
Become a stag's head. You tell me to sprinkle them
With gold dust and bring them to life.
Near you is such life
And away from you such death, and death
Because of you, appears joyful when I soar
Above the valley, heaving out of the body
Into the truer essence, instantaneously falling
Rising and moving in many directions
On the newer zone, with newer senses
New colours, awesome shapes to the sight
After traversing a Milky Way of white light
At such speed, in such a short time.

That is as much as I imagined
On this side of paradise
When the train thundered between waiting cars
At the level crossing of Coolmine station
My eyes drowned getting to a lay-by.

Your shaping flame which burns me, Jesus of women
Coming through a wall panel onto the dancefloor
Outshining your jewels
Observing from a diethylamide haze
Yet introspective.
Give me this day my daily acid burning
From synapse to synapse
Keeping the cellular stairs dusted.
I want to tell you everything that can be said
O matchless one, smoking or non-smoking?
Caressing the music and the air
Laughing at yourself for serious steps
Then serious faced at hanging loose
Stiffening every mudra, reeling into fulsomeness
The bacchanal when opaque talk is broken
Into playful inoffensive chunks of nonsense
With other layers of meaning
When you're above, casting out what is below
When you're the nightsky, city lights
As far as thought can reach
The texture of all minds and their actions
In short, I find god in you
And fuck it all, ease, a feast of hashish
And what might be. Let's go to the garden
Of delightful play among the wine fountains
And feast near the maze of shops and streets

Music and company, last night's fun
The moments by the weir when a bus
Passed beyond the high wall and your
Hand rested on my shoulder and we talked
Much closer than we stood face to face
As if no before and after would succeed
That time emblazoned in some forever.
Believe in my imaginary altar to you
Out there in the rambling city
Where rainbows girder the sky
After rain, and sun shafts the helices
And lozenges of the heavenly dome.
Surely you whose veins are in flood
of which the greater essence is of
Some imperishable spark
Sleep well in the mountains
But come home to the valley soon and steel
The will with plans and schemes
Break in a passionate phrase
'How is every tiny particle of you to-night?'
I am fine thinking of you to-night
The full moon's a photo developing its face
And long to hear you
And sit across from you

The Entertainer

❦

Brandon M. Crose

B OB WAS A HEAVYSET MAN, probably in his late forties, with pasty skin and thinning grey hair wet with sweat. He wore thick, square glasses, and an extra-large Hawaiian shirt with khaki shorts and sandals over his bandaged feet. The nasal—almost reedy—voice of Bob suited the image of Bob perfectly, but I wondered about his eyebrows. They were sparse and stubbled; almost nonexistent. Did he pluck them? *Shave* them? Why?

'We're not there yet, but I'm going to hit the music,' Bob said, then flicked a switch and turned the volume knob. 'Just let them hear it. Give them time to look under the couch cushions for change.' Bob's signature tune was 'The Entertainer'. I smiled. The ice cream men of my youth had all employed the same four-bit ditty. I would not. I would be different.

'Here we go,' said Bob, and I braced myself between the truck's freezer and the open sales window as Bob took a sharp left turn, slowed the truck to a five mile-per-hour crawl, lowered the music and deployed the flashing CAUTION sign in a series of deft, punchy motions. He drummed the steering wheel with his thumbs and waggled his non-eyebrows at me through the rear-view mirror. 'Now,' he said, 'the fun begins.'

I met Bob for the first time earlier that morning, in the gravelled parking lot of Mr. Frosty, Inc.'s southern Maine branch office. It was a breezy-warm day in early June and I had arrived for my first day

of work. 'They don't hurt at all,' he told me—meaning his bandaged feet—while he demonstrated the most efficient way to inte-
grate new boxes of ice cream into an already packed freezer. 'But
I guess that was the problem.'

As Bob told it, he had been standing barefoot in his black tar driveway, washing his ice cream truck on a sunny day barely one week
ago. He was outside for an hour before he smelled something cooking. Bob went inside to investigate—his wife was not home, he had-
n't put anything on the stove—and soon realized that he was track-
ing bloody footsteps all over his trailer's off-white carpet. He wrapped
towels around his feet and drove the truck thirty miles to the nearest
hospital, where an intern blanched and had to excuse herself after seeing Bob's feet. He had given himself first and second-degree burns.

'And you didn't feel it?' I asked, blanching a little myself.

'My nerve-endings down there don't work too well,' he
answered, slicing a hand-sized hole into a box of Rocket Pops.
'Took too many drugs when I was your age.'

I wanted to laugh but sensed that Bob was serious. *Drugs?* Surely
not. Whatever the cause, his feet did not bother him, apart from the
small matter of charred tissue. In fact, if the doctor had not threat-
ened serious surgery, Bob would have continued to drive his truck
seven days a week, ten in the morning until eight in the evening, just
as he'd done for the past six years. My presence—I was to become
Bob's part-time alternate driver—signified a certain surrender on his
part, but though he resented the whole scenario, he liked me just fine.

'Ooh,' Bob said now, pulling the truck to a stop in front of
someone's lawn. 'You get to meet the Banjo People.'

'Banjo People?'

'That's if they come out today. This should be their week.'

The house was a small one-story shadowed by large trees. The
windows were dark and appeared to be covered with brown grocery
bags. 'Are they musicians?' I asked.

'My personal theory,' said Bob, 'is that they're waiting for the
apocalypse. They come out once every two weeks to buy about
thirty dollars of ice cream from me. Otherwise, I've never seen them

leave the house. They probably have a whole stockpile of heavy weaponry and ice cream in there.'

I laughed. 'But why 'Banjo People'?'

'He doesn't shave and she doesn't talk. I don't think either of them shower. Whenever I see them, I start humming Dueling Banjos to myself. *Ba-na-now-new-now-new-now-new-nowwww*.'

Bob let 'The Entertainer' wash over their home-*cum*-barricade, and when they didn't come out after a few minutes, we continued down the street. I would not meet the Banjo People that day.

We coasted up and down the small neighborhood. This was an area I didn't know well, and so I took note of where Bob turned and which streets he passed up. It reminded me of a frivolous exercise my grade school Math teacher would give the class just before summer vacation; something having to do with tracing every line between points without marking the same line twice.

Bob stopped for two teenage girls and their Golden Retriever, who ran frantic circles around their legs, then abruptly sat down when I appeared at the window.

'You're on, Studs,' said Bob.

'Hi,' I said to the girls, who were clearly too young for me, whatever Bob might have been implying. 'What can I get you?' I made a grandiose sweeping gesture that included all of the various frozen goodies that could be theirs, while I tried to remember where everything was. First compartment, nondescript bars and pops; second compartment, cartoon faces; third compartment, cookie sandwiches and cones. Candies and pops on the shelves, a few varied cans of soda hidden in the rear. Got it.

'Just a Frosty Treat for Rex here,' one girl said, indicating the Golden Retriever, who lost his composure at the words 'Frosty Treat.' He remained sitting, but his legs shook from the effort of keeping still, and he started emitting a succession of soft yelps.

I looked helplessly at Bob, who was laughing.

'Third compartment, pink box. Two-fifty,' he said.

I peeled back the third lid and located a small, pink box. It sported a drawing of a wide-eyed grinning dog, with the words 'Frosty Treats!'

emblazoned above. And below: *Ice cream for dogs!* This had to be some kind of joke. I opened the box and removed one very small cup.

'Um,' I said, presenting the cup to the girls, 'Two-fifty please.'

One paid while the other removed the cap and placed the open cup before Rex, who, I think, wept hot tears of joy as he began assaulting the diminutive snack with his large tongue. I watched this in disbelief, and then gave the girl her change.

'What was that all about?' I asked, once they were gone.

'I buy them myself for three bucks a box at the wholesale club. There's four servings, so I make seven bucks profit on 'em. Not bad, huh?'

'But,' I said, 'they make ice cream for *dogs*?'

'Why not? They make ice cream for vegans.'

'What's in it?'

'I dunno,' said Bob. 'Probably ice cream.'

We completed the neighborhood without further sales and headed to the next route, where, Bob promised, we would have to fend off business with a stick. He told me about his own dog, Buster, who used to ride in the truck until he nipped at a girl some weeks ago. Now Buster stayed home when Bob worked, though, I observed, Buster's sleeping mat remained.

'You'll understand if you ever see this girl,' Bob said. 'Animals are very perceptive beings, and Buster sensed the evil within.'

I tried to get a reading on Bob. Again, he was serious.

'She used to come to the truck and stare at me. Wouldn't say anything, but you could see the hellfire burning in her eyes.'

'How old is she?' I asked.

'Oh, eight or nine, maybe. Anyway, she'd just stare at me. Ordered nothing, wouldn't say yes, she had money, or no, she did not; didn't speak a word when I finally drove away. Just stared.'

'Weird,' I agreed.

'So one day Buster peeked over the window and her face just lit up. She bared her teeth, thrust her hand at Buster, and snarled, '*Puppy!*'' Here Bob affected a demonic little-girl voice. 'Buster's no fool. He growled at her. Then the girl grabbed the windowsill with both hands and started to pull herself through the window, still snarling 'Puppy, puppy, puppy!' So Buster nipped at her.'

'What happened?'

'Well, the girl shrieked and ran home. Her mother came out and yelled at me a bit. I tried to point out that the girl was threatening Buster, but of course she wouldn't hear it. I mean, who's she going to believe: her little psychotic whelp, or the ice cream man?'

'Yeah,' I said, assuming the question was rhetorical.

'Anyway, she called the company boss-man, who told me that Buster couldn't ride with me anymore. He didn't even break the skin! Buster's a loyal friend, but he's all bark,' he said, proudly.

'You're lucky that her mother didn't call the police,' I said.

'The police probably know all about this girl. Here's the best part: now, whenever the girl hears me coming, she gets on her bicycle and chases me all around the neighborhood, screaming, 'I hate you! I hate you!' You can almost see the twin horns, dripping fangs, and bat wings. Crazy demon-girl.'

'Is Buster a fan of the Frosty Treats?' I asked.

'Is he ever!' Bob chuckled. 'I've seen plenty of heroin addicts go through withdrawal, and it was nothing compared to the shakes Buster had when I cut him off from the Frosty Treats. He got all snappy and irrational. Rex back there is in for a hard time, I think.' The truck decelerated and Bob flipped on 'The Entertainer'. 'Almost there,' he said.

We entered a larger neighborhood where, as promised, unwashed legions of children swarmed the ice cream truck. Bob, bemused by my panic, remained in the driver's seat and told me where certain hard-to-find confections could be found, while I, breathless and baffled, tried to establish something approximating order within the unruly mob. When that failed, I began handing out whatever they asked for, no matter how rudely they asked for it, and took whatever money they gave me, hoping that it would all even out afterwards. What seemed like hours later, and once all children had departed with a rapidly melting treat in their sweaty palms, I collapsed against the freezer and cast Bob a baleful look.

'Good job,' he said.

'They kicked my ass,' I replied.

'Guess you'll have to learn to kick theirs back,' Bob said. 'After all, *you're* the ice cream man.' He gave me a jocular thumbs-up and put the truck into gear, continuing our slow exploration of then-unfamiliar terrain that I would, by summer's end, know intimately.

Later, over lunch, Bob grew philosophical:

'Y'know,' he said, around a mouthful of convenience store-bought egg salad, 'now that you're gonna be an Ice Cream Man, you ought to give some thought to what you'll be thinking about all summer. Lacking the good company of a starry-eyed trainee'—and here he winked at me—'to be The Ice Cream Man is to be alone with your thoughts for most of the day. What you think about during those long hours might save you from going nuts. Depending, that is, on what you're thinkin' about.'

'What do you think about?'

'Oh,' Bob looked at the truck's white ceiling, where the paint was flaking in some spots, 'I guess I think about the people I've met, the stories they've told me. You would not believe the crazy stuff you hear on this truck.' He opened a bag of potato chips and chewed on them contemplatively. 'Maybe I'll write them all down someday.'

'You should,' I said, but he didn't seem to hear me. We finished our lunches.

'And I'll tell ya something else,' Bob finally said, as we pulled away from the gas station parking lot, 'you will meet some girls on this job. *Girls*, my friend. Old acquaintances, older sisters, even young mothers. They all have fond memories of the ice cream man, and a guy like you could have some serious fun this summer.'

I chuckled uneasily and did not ask him to elaborate. Perhaps there was a story, but I preferred not to hear it.

'Serious fun,' Bob repeated, more to himself than to me.

We continued the day in companionable silence, Bob occasionally illustrating the perils of sharp turns, the necessity of riding the brake even while coasting through kid-heavy neighbourhoods at very low speeds, the superiority of 'The Entertainer' over any of the other available tunes (at an approximate length of thirteen seconds, it had the longest playing time; an obvious virtue). I gained a working familiarity with the locations and prices of the merchandise, and even sampled the most expensive items at Bob's urging. Noting his substantial heft, I resolved not to make a habit of this.

As day gave way to dusk, Bob flipped more switches. The truck's interior bulbs flickered on, and a rotating light on top of the truck whirled to life. I watched our bright reflection ghost by in darkened windows, the beacon light illuminating the neighborhood in circular sweeps. In the near-darkness, 'The Entertainer' sounded false, tinny; almost like a distant intruder alarm.

'Got another one,' Bob said. 'Then we'll head back.'

'Sure,' I said, stifling a yawn.

'A bit of a cautionary tale for you, so pay careful attention.'

'Okay,' I said.

'Well, I've been driving this truck for six summers now, and I've gotta tell ya, some of the other drivers are pretty wacko. Granted, I'm not exactly your average Joe, but these guys…'

We stopped for two boys and their father. I sold bubblegum bars to the kids and a chocolate éclair to the father, after which I gave them all a jaunty wave to offset the weird twilight feeling of selling ice cream at dark hours. They left, and Bob continued:

'Anyway, the constant solitude of this job can warp a person's mind after awhile, and one of the other drivers—this was during my first summer on the truck, by the way—got sick of it and started taking a boom box with him, playing his own music so that he wouldn't have to hear 'The Entertainer' reverberating in his skull all day. Something loud but classy, like opera.'

'Sounds reasonable,' I said.

'Sure. But here's the thing: his business waned, and he began to worry that the music was to blame. Maybe he couldn't hear the kids yelling for him to stop. So he kept an ear open, and sure enough, just barely over the singing fat lady, he heard kids screaming. But when he turned down the music and stopped the truck, there was no one there.'

'The neighborhood was entirely empty?'

'Well, I mean that no one had yelled for him. He'd imagined it.'

'Ah.'

'This began to seriously trouble him. And worse, he was barely making enough to cover the truck's rent and gas. He began to wonder if another driver was stealing his business, possibly on the next street over, and he couldn't hear his competitor's jingle because of the opera music. And then, of course, he began to hear someone else's 'Entertainer' echoing back at him. But when he turned the music down, he only heard his own jingle.'

'Why didn't he get rid of the boom box?'

'Because then he would have gone really crazy. We're talking about a guy who had been driving the same routes and listening to the same thirteen-second tune for nearly ten summers. He needed something to take his mind off the job.'

'Okay,' I said, wondering how many summers it takes before reflecting upon other people's crazy stories doesn't cut it anymore.

'So finally, one day, he glimpses the backside of the competitor's truck turning a corner just as he pulls onto an empty street. He's got the guy, right? He blares his horn and accelerates, makes it halfway up the street and just barely sees a sudden flash of blonde hair and a small hand as someone's kid goes under his truck. He knows it's too late, but he swerves and screeches to a halt, flips the truck, sends the freezer through the sales window and his boxes of ice cream and jars of candy all over the pavement. Bleeding and dazed, he crawls out through the busted up windshield… but there was no kid.'

'Jesus,' I said. 'What happened?'

'He quit that same day and left the truck lying sideways in the middle of the street. Last I heard, he'd landed himself in the psycho ward of Maine Med. That was a couple of years ago. I don't know where he is now.'

'Wow,' I said. We finished the route in silence, and then Bob took us back to the lot, where he showed me how to plug in the truck's freezer and where to hide the cashbox at night. He locked the truck, handed the keys to me, and shook my hand. 'We'll switch off every other day, so she's yours tomorrow,' he said. 'Good luck.'

'Bob, wait. About that last story.'

'Yeah?'

'Well, what was I supposed to take from it?'

'Take from it?'

'You said it was a cautionary tale. What's the lesson? Don't play your own music while working? Don't speed?'

Bob ran his hand through the remaining wisps on his head and shrugged. 'I guess. Take what you want out of it. It's just a story.'

Trying to favor the cooked soles of his nerveless feet, Bob tiptoed to his car and settled heavily into it with a groan. He turned the ignition and music—an aria of some kind—trilled from the car's speakers. I watched his tail-lights recede and then began walking home, past the silent row of parked ice cream trucks, through the darkened neighborhoods of my old hometown, already planning how I would drive my ice cream truck this summer. I decided that I would play 'The Entertainer,' too.

The Boat Train

Eithne McGuinness

MY SISTER RAN AWAY when I was fourteen years old. She stopped talking after the police took her home, even to me. In the dead of night her crying woke me; she wouldn't stop until I crawled down the end of my bed and reached across the darkness. She had beautiful hair. One morning she simply wasn't there. Nobody said anything. The following Sunday, my father rose at dawn. I kneeled on my bed to watch him reverse out of the driveway, then climbed shivering into the warm patch he'd left behind. My mother grunted.

'Where's Daddy gone?'

'To look for Orla, go back to sleep.'

He didn't find her.

'London's a big place,' he said when he came home.

I imagined him searching train stations, alleys and lanes, like the bald fella in *The Sweeney*. Shaking tramps awake, her photograph cupped in his palm. Quizzing down-and-outs and crazy people and drunks. Jumping off red double-decker buses to chase misleading heads of gold. He went again two weeks later, came back late on Sunday evening, sat silently holding my mother's hand. His eyes, worn out from searching, retreated into his head.

I started wearing her coat. It still smelled of patchouli and cigarettes. My mother had bought it in the Arnotts' sale—twenty-four ninety-nine. Navy blue, three buttons, big blue ones with a white line around the edge and a double lapel, also edged in white. A nipped waist with a skirt that swung when I walked, it used to have a belt but my mother said Orla had no waist so she threw it out. It was the most fashionable thing I had ever worn. I never took it off, even in the house; drove my mother mad.

'You look ridiculous. It does nothing for you. There isn't even any heat in it. Put your duffle coat on.'

Nobody said anything at the new school. To be honest, I didn't go in much. After Orla left, I got expelled from my real school. I spent two months watching *Open University* and *The Magic Roundabout* in the afternoons. I hadn't done anything really bad, just stopped going to classes. It was because they wouldn't answer my questions, said I was to pay attention to the matter in hand. They didn't seem to understand that I had to start at the beginning of things, so that the middle made sense. Dundrum Vocational School finally agreed to take me in. By then, I'd got used to not having friends.

One Monday morning, the number seventeen was late. Spitting rain turned my coat the colour of a wet crow's wing. At Dundrum the driver—Jimmy was his name—pulled in, though no one rang the bell.

'Dundrum,' he said, at the top of his voice, as if I didn't know. Two oul wans turned around for a good stare. I huddled deeper into the back left hand seat. He wouldn't speak to me when I got off at the terminus; he hated it when I didn't go to school.

In the train station, Mr. Byrne sat to the right of the stove, a game of Patience neatly spread out on the low table.

'Will I make the tea?'

'Do.'

I went in the back, filled the kettle and washed two cups; white, with thin green bands and golden harps. Scalded the pot and put in three heaped spoons of tea. Poured boiling water over the leaves and covered the pot with the brown cozy that Mr. Byrne's wife made. He said it used to be yellow. Put everything on a tray: cups, the bag of sugar—lumpy from sticking wet spoons into it. A bottle of milk that the birds had been at, and an open packet of custard creams. Mr. Byrne took two sugars and a drop of milk after the tea was poured. I was off sugar for Lent and I preferred my milk in first.

'Tea in your milk, more like. Hang up your coat over the stove, let it dry out.'

I looked away.

'Well, sit in beside the fire then. Catch your end.'

He dunked his biscuit; a yellow swirl rose glinting to the surface of the tea. He gave the cards a good shuffle, dealt out a game of Switch, and turned over a card: the queen of diamonds. I played the two.

'No pity, no pity at all for a poor old man.'

He played the two of clubs.

I was picking up four cards when the door flew open. A black-haired fella in a donkey jacket; leather patches on the shoulders and arms. Silver buttons, stamped Coras Iompar Eireann, dangling. Raindrops hung from the thick hank of hair over his right eye. I had a strange urge to go over and fix it for him. Staring at me from under the brim of his cap, he smiled and pushed the door to. I tried to smile back, but my mouth wouldn't work—my lip got stuck on my gums.

'Get in here and play a hand with us. The tea is getting cold.'

He pulled over a stool, sat right by me and stuck out his hand.

'Liam.'

I rolled my tongue up, loosened my lip, but couldn't speak.

'This here is Isabel, she comes to visit sometimes.'

I got up and fetched him a cup.

Mr. Byrne shuffled and dealt out three hands.

It was in to Liam. He played a seven, skipping me.

I played one back.

'This one is trouble.'

I laughed.

'I'll have to watch me step.'

We played a few games. I lost them all; no concentration. The cargo train went through. Liam went out to do the flags. We played Forty-Fives. I lost again. Mr. Byrne read the paper. Liam opened the door of the stove and sat looking into the fire. The humming of the rails signalled the approach of the one ten; I went into the back. Perched on the wooden fence around the coal, I counted passengers through a crack in the door. Six dripping women, three with umbrellas; all bar one hoiking shopping bags. Five boys from Marian College wearing caps; home for dinner, their blazers soaked through, a red-and-white crest on the pocket. They'd be back in forty minutes. Between one and two was our busiest time.

I knew the boat train was well gone by the time I got in, but I liked to check every train, just in case. She might have felt like a walk on the pier after all the dirty air in London, or she could have bumped into Auntie Helen who lived out that way in a flat. She would definitely get out here; the seventeen bus stop was right outside the door. I hoped she hadn't forgotten that—she might be confused with all the different buses over there. Da didn't have to hit her so hard; he'd never hit either of us before. My mother did the hitting in our house. He wasn't there much; got up at six and only came home for dinner on Saturdays and Sundays when holy hour was on and there wasn't a lock-in down at the pub. Saturdays he gave us pocket money and on Sundays he fell asleep as soon as he was fed.

He banged her up against the wardrobe, knocking the door off its gliders, shouting his head off about swimming in the nude and the shame of it; police knocking on the door and hanging around with butchers, and he wasn't going to waste his hard-earned money on college fees if she was going to lower herself with un-educated louts who got decent people out of their beds at this hour. He ended each sentence with a clout. When she fell on the floor, he dragged her up by the hair and hissed into her face.

'Stay away from that joker with his motorbike and his smarty-pants dial or I tell you; I won't be responsible.'

'His name is Matthew,' she screamed as he locked the door.

Afterwards, she crawled into my bed. I laid my arm carefully across her middle in case I'd land on a bruise. Next morning I asked,

'Were you doing it when they caught you?'

She made a funny sound, halfway between a sob and a laugh.
'Were you?'
'We were fucking floating… counting stars.'
That was the last thing she ever said to me.

The Marian boys were back, faces puce from rushing. I leafed
through the rules and regulations book, then tidied the stacks of
tickets: pink, orange and green. Brand new; they smelled like sher-
bet. I thought of stealing some. I could treat Orla to the bumper
cars in Bray when she came home.

Liam leaned up against the doorjamb, jacket off. I could hardly
see his face; the sun was out, grazing his head. A white collar, stiff
against his neck; envelope points tucked in under the band of his
tight ribbed jumper. I sat back on the fence.

'You need more coal.'

He came close, peeped over my shoulder. 'I'll take a note.'

'Do.'

He kissed me without any warning, right there in the back
room, beside the coal, with passengers coming and going and Mr.
Byrne getting ready to close down the hatch. I kissed him back,
the way Orla had showed me on the back of her arm. He started
foostering with one of the big buttons on my coat. I moved his
hand to my back, like she said, but like a blind puppy it wound its
way back to my front. Giving up on the buttons, which were good
and stiff, he put his hand inside my coat and squeezed. I tried to
remember the rules: upstairs outside was ok, but downstairs was
not. Was this still outside, if it was inside your coat? What were the
rules for kissing strangers in a train station in the afternoon?

The fingers of his other hand were suddenly stroking the inside
of my thigh. I hadn't even noticed them till now; too busy paying
attention to my breast. I knew this was out of bounds, certainly on
a first date or whatever this was. Jamming my knees together, I
opened my eyes. His were closed, a kind of sleepy look on his face.

He seemed separated from his corkscrewing fingers; they pawed the softest part of my skin. I had a sudden longing for my sister. I promised myself if she ever came home I'd make her write a list, so I would know exactly what to do. I'd make her tell me everything so I'd be ready the next time she went away. If we were alone, and it was dark and she wasn't crying too much.

His thumb lifted the elastic of my knickers, I felt cold air, his nail scraped my skin. Mr. Byrne coughed directly outside the door. Dave let me go and started to fill the kettle. I stayed where I was. Mr. Byrne looked happy to see me smile.

'Lunchtime.'

I could still feel his imprint; steamy patches on my flesh, felt such a craving for his fingertips now that they were gone.

Liam had batch loaf with thick slices of Hazlet in a Tupperware box.

'Banker's sandwiches,' Mr. Byrne said. 'The wife looks after him well.'

He took his bread and marmalade out of the pocket of his overcoat, wrapped, as usual, in a Johnston, Mooney and O'Brien wrapper. We ate in silence. I found it hard to swallow my Jacobs cream crackers, scalded my mouth on the tea. Mr. Byrne got me a drink of water. Liam went out onto the platform, climbed up onto the wall overlooking the baths, sat staring into nothing. The wall was too high for me to climb. I stood on the footbridge. A black raincloud was working its way north from Dunlaoghaire. The green sea was turning grey under a sky the colour of tarmacadam. It started to drizzle so I went inside.

Mr. Byrne settled in beside the fire and dealt out a hand of Patience.

'Can I play?'

'I'm expectin' the supervisor.'

'I thought he came on Wednesdays.'

'Go on, off with ye like a good girl, do what you're told.'

'What's Liam doing here anyway?'

'And don't come back this week now, d'ya hear? You'll get us all into trouble.'

That night I couldn't sleep; I wore my coat to bed, nothing else, just the coat. Practised opening and closing the buttons. Between my legs was hot and sticky, I felt all jittery. I pulled back the curtains to look for stars; nothing but clouds.

Next morning, Liam was in the hatch, stamping tickets.

'Where's Mr. Byrne?'

'Holidays.'

'How long?'

'A week.'

All that week I stayed close to him. He would look at me steadily, then slowly drop his eyelids till I could see the crease. We played cards. I started to win. He didn't care. I stood behind him while he read the paper; once I rubbed his shoulders the way Orla had taught me. He let a whimper out of him, tried to cover it with a cough. When I rested my breasts on the curve of his neck, he scratched my cheek with his three-day beard as he pulled away. I could smell his breath; onions and custard creams.

On Wednesday I hid in the lane that led to Blackrock Park, waiting for the supervisor to arrive. I waited all day and he never came. Liam waved at me when he was out doing the flags, but he wouldn't come anywhere close to where I swung off the railings.

'First day of Spring,' I told my mother when I woke her to get my bus money on Thursday. She grunted. Since Orla went away, she didn't get up till lunchtime. At the station, Liam smiled when I stuck my head around the door. He made tea and studied the leavings in my cup.

'You're going to marry a man in uniform and move to Australia.'

'You're making that up.'

'That's what it says in the tea leaves, Isabel, clear as day.'

He said his granny taught him because he was the eldest and divining skipped a generation. She was known to have 'the touch' the length and breadth of Wexford.

On Friday I got up early and had a bath. I put on a red peasant skirt that Orla had left behind. It was a bit long, even for a maxi; I rolled the waistband up and rooted out her old cork platforms;

they had a hole cut out of the heel. The wardrobe door still didn't close. I dabbed *Charlie* behind my ears, then put on my coat. My mother sat up in the bed. She laughed.

'What on earth are you wearing? Is it fancy dress today?'

I slammed the door.

Liam nodded at the skirt as he threw a shovel of coal on the fire.

'Going somewhere special?'

'Maybe.'

'You wouldn't want it to get messed up in here.'

I took off my coat, hoping he could see my nipples through the cheesecloth blouse. He dealt a hand of Whist.

'Nice colour, red.'

'It's my sister's.'

'Oh.'

'She ran away.'

'Oh?'

'To London.'

'Great city.'

'Is it?'

'The best.'

'She'll come home on the boat.'

'Indeed'n she will, or you can pay her a visit on your way to Australia.'

After the lunchtime rush, he found me scouring the square white sink with Ajax in the back room.

'You'll get housewife's hands.'

'I don't care.'

He was so close. I felt his warmth along the knobs of my spine. He caught my earlobe in his teeth. I leaned back. He took my hand

and put it on his thing. It was hot, thumping against the cloth of his trousers. I patted it, remembering the mouse Orla won at a sale of work when I was ten. She called him Oscar. He struggled against my palms all the way to Bushy Park, where Mammy threw him under a hedge.

Matthew hadn't gone with Orla like she said in the note; I checked. He was still there in Simpson's Butchers hacking at bones.

My hand slipped. Liam pulled away. I turned around to find him with my coat in his hands.

'You're a lovely girl. Go home.'

He put my arms into my sleeves, closed the buttons one by one and, ignoring my tears, pushed me gently through the door.

My Golden Puppet

Roisín Boyd

My father was reading to me when they came, the way he reads to me every evening after we have had our supper. My little sister Blessing was playing and gurgling with her toes. Papa says she does not understand the stories he reads to me yet. But I think that maybe she does understand, because she laughs at the same time that Papa and I laugh.

This night, we could see the stars glinting outside the window. There are no panes of glass in our window-frame, and Papa says we are lucky, because that means we get all the benefit when the breezes ripple in from the Indian Ocean. The pages of the storybook rustle when the breeze comes and then Papa says,

'Tiku, will you please hold down the page.' I put my fingers carefully at the edge of the page.

My father was reading me his favourite tales when the soldiers came to take him away. I am sure you would like to know the name of his favourite story because it is my favourite one too. It is called

'Alice's Adventures in Wonderland.' Papa told me to always remember this story. He said that the people in our country should read this story too.

He did not stop reading to me, even when we heard the loud knocks on the door.

My mother stopped wringing out my clothes. I love watching her curl the wet cotton into thick snakes of cloth. She was getting them ready for my school next morning. My little sister Blessing, she even stopped laughing. Our parrot Klondike stopped his 'Who's a naughty boy then? Who's a naughty boy then?'

But my father didn't stop reading and I listened to him read, even though my legs were stiff and there were pins and needles in my hand. I didn't move or shift my position. I was rigid like my puppet.

Splinters from the door of our hut flew across the room like darts, when the soldiers rammed their rifles into the thin wood. I smelt the eucalyptus sap from the wood. The soldiers were shouting, 'Open up. Open up.'

They said it in our language but you don't understand that so I will tell you what they said in English. They said a lot of other bad things too but I don't think I remember those things.

My father continued to read. I stared at the door where there was now an enormous hole. I could see the soldiers and the stars and the bats swoop, through the gap in the door. My father admonished me.

'Tiku,' he said, 'are you listening to our story?'

I said, 'Yes I am listening, Papa.'

I told a lie.

My mother was holding my dripping school shirt in front of her with both her hands still. The front of her dress was wet now. I wanted to shout, 'Mama, Mama, look—you are wetting the floor.'

But I couldn't speak. Now I understood I had lost my tongue. That's what my teacher said to me in class, when I could not remember the answers to his question:

'Have you lost your tongue, boy?'

The tears on my mother's face were diamonds. They sparkled on her eyelashes, on her cheeks, and on her chin.

The soldiers shouted 'Stop, stop.'

My father ignored them even when they pushed their rifles into his eyes. I saw his blood dropping onto 'Alice in Wonderland'.

But when they struck his mouth and his lips cracked and his teeth broke, he had to stop then. I heard the crunch of enamel on metal and smelt the cold iron from the gun and the hot iron from his blood.

He stopped reading to me then. He said, 'Tiku, do not forget to tell stories. You must tell Blessing stories when I am not here. You must take care of your little sister when I am gone.'

Every day my mother scrubs the wooden pallets on the floor with bleach.

'I have to clean away the blood,' she says.

But no matter how hard she scrubs, I can still see the marks ingrained in the wood from my father's blood. Now we smell old blood and bleach every day when we wake up.

I am glad that there are pink patches to remind us of Papa, even if it's not a good memory.

Those, and the storybook and the puppet, all remind me of my father who is now far away from us.

Before they took my father he carved Sol (that is the name of my puppet) from pieces of wood we found in the rain forest. Sol's arms, which are half the size of mine, are stiff because Papa didn't have time to make the joints. His legs have joints though, and I can make him dance when I pull his strings. His strings are gold; they are magic. When I tug Sol's strings, strange things happen. Very strange and wonderful things. I will pull the strings now.

See, we are flying with Sol through the clouds; oh, I bumped into a cloud and now I have made it rain. The farmers will be very happy. Sol tells me to be careful; he says when I sit on a cloud I must take great care not to sit too heavily. I have to hold my breath because if I sit heavily, I will disappear into the cloud and I will never be seen again. It's quite tricky but Sol helped me. I think it is easier for him because he is floppy. It is the most wonderful feeling in the world to sit on a cloud. It is even softer than my mother's lap. I sink into the folds of the cloud and then my legs disappear and then they reappear. I am floating towards a place where it is neither hot nor cold, and Sol is bringing me there.

When we arrive there are three puppets waiting to meet us. I am not sure how we got there, because one minute I am sitting on the cloud, and the next Sol says, 'Close your eyes and hold your breath.'

I hear him mumbling some strange words and boom! We have arrived.

Understanding Women
Through Taxidermy

John Durnin

I PLAY SITAR just off Grafton St.

Well, I used to play in Temple Bar, but it got rather tiresome in there—a sitar is made of pumpkin gourds and if you've got a bunch of drunk guys swaying around you while you're playing, you begin to worry that one might just keel over and shatter your instrument. And sitars are hard to get. Have you ever just seen one in a store window? Sitar discount! All single gourd sitars reduced by thirty percent! I'm betting not. But I moved to the side streets off Grafton rather than Grafton St. itself because I didn't want to be one of Those People. You know, like the crazy Japanese lady or the young kids with teased hair and cheap guitars who sing *Satisfaction*. I figured that I'd tuck myself off in a corner like the old guy who plays accordion, and the other old guy with the big beard and the tin whistle. I make decent money because a lot of people have never seen a sitar before and they drop money because they think it's a sight to see. I can kind of play it, even. Whenever someone who looks like they might know a thing about sitar walks by, I'm very conscientious to stop playing and re-tune the sympathetic strings; that can take forty minutes if need be. I'll out-bore anyone I don't feel like playing for.

You get strange types when you play sitar in public. Everyone thinks you're enlightened. For instance, people will comment on the peace in my eyes, or the length of my hair; and it's nice of them, but I'm really just a guy who tries to play sitar. Sometimes people want to talk about god. I don't really have any opinions on god. God seems like a good idea, when taken in moderation and not too eagerly applied to the more minor facets of life. I had real trouble with two guys in particular—Mitch and Gary, they were theology students and they used to catch me for ten or even twenty minutes at a time, telling me how beautiful my soul was because I played sitar, how at peace I must have been, how they aspired to reach the 'level' that I had. I tried to tell them that I wasn't happy—I'd just broken up with my girlfriend, I didn't have a job, I was developing bruises on my arse from sitting on the street all day and was only playing in public with the hope that I might make a bit of money. I lost them when I moved to the side streets off Grafton. But I met Camille.

Camille dropped a whole euro in my case.

'Thank you,' I smiled and played as fast a bit as I could manage (just a scale, but even scales sound like deep music on a sitar).

'Where'd you learn to play?' asked Camille.

'Self taught.'

Camille wore a knee-length jacket. It was deep mahogany or purple with a turquoise square pattern woven into it. She wore it with brown suede boots with fringe tassels, and acorn earrings. I couldn't get over the acorn earrings—no one could make acorn earrings look like a good idea, but I didn't mind them on Camille. She smiled so confidently, as if to tease you to think less of her for wearing acorn earrings. But the way she looked at me I knew she knew I couldn't really play the sitar very well, and if she was smiling at me, she was smiling because we could meet there like that on the street and know between ourselves all the ridiculousness of playing sitar in public.

'I'm Will,' I said, holding out my hand.

'Camille.'

'Camille, I've made enough for some tea—I'd love to have some with you.'

'Sure,' said Camille. I was amazed. So much so that I forgot her name. I put my sitar away and walked with her around the corner to a café.

She had peppermint tea. Wonderful. I had peppermint tea, too.

I understood here, coming to sit at our table, that this moment was the moment of awkwardness—we had met, we'd spoken a couple of words to each other, and we'd brought ourselves here for a cup of tea. By this point mild suspicion as to *why* each of us was available for tea began to set in. But I caught myself—street performers can really only look better once you have them off the street, and I didn't see any reason for things to become awkward between us. We spent an hour talking about all manner of things —jack-o'-lanterns and our mutual dislike for them, sushi, whether red bricks or yellow bricks are more aesthetically pleasing—what she did for a living, what I used to do. Then she said,

'I was just on my way home—I'm having a friend over for dinner and I really need to start cooking. But have you been to the Natural History Museum?'

'No, I don't think I have.'

'Would you like to meet there at 12, next Sunday?'

'Sure!' I said happily. I really liked her.

'Camille,' she said, smiling. She knew I'd forgotten her name again. I fell in love with her.

All that week I dreamt of Camille. Her hair *did* bounce as we walked to the café, didn't it? I was almost certain that it had. The Natural History Museum seemed a strange place to go, but it didn't matter—what mattered was that I would get to see her again, that she had *invited me* to the museum.

She was there at twelve sharp. I was waiting outside in my best jumper, a pair of khakis and shaved face—basically the opposite way I looked the first time we'd met. I do admit that I possess that generic tidy-up instinct when meeting someone for the second time, even though the person obviously was attracted to whatever look or person I presented upon that first meeting. But no bother— she looked sweet as she approached in a similar skirt and the same fantastic jacket, and her hair *did* bounce (I was on a date with a girl with bouncy hair!).

The sun was out and we stood a moment talking outside; her

hair was right between blonde and brown in the rain, but in the sun, it was red—as I watched the light play on the highlights of her follicles, I thought this, this is what I want. She could sit cross-legged right beside me as I played on the street. I could dreadlock my hair and we could have little hippie babies—I'd grow a dark long beard if that happened. We could be completely, utterly devoted to each other. I knew it—I knew it in the soft cadence of her voice, in the way she smiled at the slightest attempt I made at superficiality.

'Let's go in and look at the animals,' she said.

'Alright, yes,' I said. Yes I said yes I said yes.

I don't like taxidermy.

At all.

At all at all.

I don't know what I thought I'd find in the museum—a natural history museum, I expected maybe skeletons, maybe long infor-mation screens and cross sections of elm trees. When I met the Hippopotamus, shot, stuffed and sealed, circa 1888, I felt the first wave of nausea. But not my brave Camille.

'Look at the zipper on him!' she exclaimed, pointing to the long, endless incision that had been made along the poor thing's stomach.

The polar bear had seven bullet holes that I could count.

'Why would they keep shooting him?' I asked Camille weakly.

'They must have been pretty scared—polar bears *are* the most vicious creatures on the planet, you know.'

I stared into the polar bear's eyes. They were made of glass.

'Come on,' she said, 'the bugs are next!'

We spent half an hour opening and closing small wooden cabi-nets, each like Pandora's box, and inside each were microscopic fleas, ticks—a hypochondriac's nightmare, all pinned to white linen sheets. I comforted myself thinking this was the end of the exhibit.

'We'll go upstairs next,' Camille said. 'I don't know if we'll make it to the fourth floor today—we might have to come back to see all the things in the jars, but we definitely need to see the whale!'

'Do you come here often?' I asked her.

'I came here *all the time* as a child. My father would bring me. In fact, he used to leave me here and go around to the pub—I never had to go back to get him! I'd spend hours looking at all the animals, a lot of them are extinct today.'

'Probably that monkey whose head was shaped like a moon... I wonder why they tried to preserve dormice?'

'To be thorough,' Camille answered matter-of-factly.

I found myself next in a long gallery with a whale hanging overhead—a mess of zippers, glass eyes, and what was most likely flaking skin after nearly one hundred years hanging in the gallery hall. They had the whale roped up on pulleys and thick coarse rope; a harness stretched under its belly. I wondered if there were steel beams run through it for support.

'Amazing isn't it?' Camille asked, placing a hand on my chest as she looked up at the corrugated underbelly of the beast. I looked into her eyes and saw only delight, fascination, even love. Nausea overtook me.

I had the sensation of tiny bits of that ancient whale's skin in my nose, being sucked into my lungs, pressing their way into my bloodstream—I was contaminated with a dead whale's dusty spores and skin flakes. I didn't want Camille any more. All I wanted was to be home.

I made a hasty, ridiculous exit. I complained that I was feeling feverish and that when I feel feverish, which I don't often do but sometimes it happens, that I generally need to go home and lie down for a bit and while it isn't anything serious, it *is* something that I should see after and take care of—no no, don't feel sorry, I'll be alright. I just need to lie down at home when I feel feverish; maybe mono or something like that, haha. It took me a good five minutes to make my goodbye speech.

I left alone under the giant antlers of ancient mammoth Irish deer, not even waiting for Camille to see me out the door.

I laid in bed all that evening thinking about Camille; about how beautiful she had appeared to me, about how much I hated the sight of that poor polar bear with the eleven bullet holes, the giant sperm whale roped to the ceiling of the gallery. I thought about how beautiful the skeleton of that whale would have appeared, like the ceilings' own rafters—but imagining the flesh, sealed in wax and other agents, still clinging to the bones of the thing, I felt more heartbroken than I had when my girlfriend left me. What was worse, was that whenever I thought of myself and Camille, I could only picture us in one of those glass diorama boxes, zippers all up and down our torsos with glass eyes stuck in our sockets and stuffed pigeons in our mouths, the label reading 'Homo Sapiens in their Natural Environment.'

I didn't play sitar in the streets for several days, for fear that Camille would try to find me. I didn't want to see her.

I felt composed again, but angry at Camille as well. If I had had a month, just a month to get to know her, I could have handled the taxidermy fascination. I hadn't insisted on taking her to a comic bookstore, or to a Stanley Kubrick film festival, or a guitar store, had I? Who was she to throw taxidermy at me on a first date? Some people introduce you to their parents too quickly—Camille had a family made up of poached mammals arranged with *papier mâché* moss in glass cabinets. She had grown up with them. In the early hours of lonely mornings I would try to reason with myself; were they any different from the stuffed animals I had played with as a child? If I took Camille on a tour of my attic, would it look all that different?

Self-doubt would creep in by midday. I hadn't wanted to understand Camille. That's why I rejected the museum. I had been dreaming of a woman without a museum, without taxidermic friends. And now when I had found the perfect woman (bouncing hair, a mahogany jacket, peppermint tea) I had rejected her because she had a few preserved dormice in her retinue.

I returned to playing sitar on the streets on weekends, but it wasn't the same. The great whale had contaminated me. My fingers shook when attempting to bend notes; I made less money. People could see it in my eyes. I imagined the men walking by would have killed for the chance to go to the Natural History Museum with Camille, and I had thrown it all away. I had stood under the giant whale with her hand pressed against my chest and fled from perfection when all it asked of me was that I smile at some animal corpses. Or rather return the smiles that the corpses' lips were pulled into.

Or I could have been honest. 'Camille, I don't really like taxidermy.' If I'd been brazen enough to own up to my hesitation, she might have even said she didn't like it either. Maybe we would have gone to a pub instead. We could have laughed about how ridiculous a first date a Natural History museum was.

'Something to tell our children,' Camille would laugh, and then blush red and duck her head.

'I was just thinking that,' I'd smile. Then she'd look up and we would have been as good as married. Logistically, I was hours away from marrying Camille when I fled the museum.

❧

I froze mid-raga whenever I saw a coat like Camille's (you can't really make any kind of graceful escape when you have a sitar across your lap) but she never passed by my perch again. Gary and Mitch found me though.

'Here you are, man o' man—you left Temple,' they said, but they seemed puzzled by something.

'You look worried,' said Gary.

'You look tense,' said Mitch. 'Like you dropped a level.'

They dropped twenty cents in my case and waved goodbye. I gathered up my coins.

What Remains

(extract from a novel)

Patrick Finnegan

Maeve Gallagher is exasperated. Her mother can be such an inconsiderate bitch. Does she have absolutely no clue at all? Did she not think Maeve would have more things on her mind today? Why of course Maeve, successful investment banker, superwoman and daughter, i.e. slave at every beck and call, would be able to provide chauffeur service for her younger sister Aoife *and* get a smear test done in the one morning. Aoife has just returned from an orchestra trip in England and is now sitting beside Maeve in the waiting room of Dr Murphy's clinic. Maeve tugs at a strand of her long blonde hair. This is not how she planned it. She should have gone for this examination back in Dublin. Then again, the familiarity of here, Ballyburn, will make it easier. Yes, that's how she should look at it.

Maeve dreads what is lined up before her this morning. But she has chosen it. She has to go through with it. When she was younger she used to worry that people would discover *It*, that she would be exposed and her character tarnished. She is twenty-five years old now, it should be less of an issue. She hopes it will be; she has never hoped for something quite so much.

Damn her mother—she should know better, she knows the importance of such screenings: cancer has torn strips from both sides of her family tree, she herself has had two scares. But Maeve isn't really getting this examination done for cancer-screening purposes.

She is testing herself—to see how far she has come, to see if there is a chance she will ever feel some semblance of normality. She needs to get on with her life. She needs to put *It* as far behind her as possible. She needs to be focussed. She needs to be on top of her game. She should be concentrating, strategising against herself and what will ensue. But the sixteen year old Aoife is in a state of animation, distracting her with stupid stuff.

'Then Miss Connors, the wrinkly old bitch, found a condom in Siobhan O'Hare's violin case and she went ape-shit. Everyone reckons Connors is a frigid—'

'Jesus, Aoife! Will—you—just—stop?' Maeve whispers, conscious of the old age pensioners seated around them in the claustrophobic room. 'My head is nearly gone from listening to you.'

Aoife is cut by this; she continuously tries to impress her older sister. 'What's up your arse?' she snaps, not caring about discretion.

'Well, give me twenty minutes and I'll be able to tell ya exactly what'll be stuck up me.'

'Ewwww, Maeve!'

'Go on out to the car. Wait for me there. And don't have the radio or CD player on. You'll run the battery down.'

'I want to stay here and keep you company.'

'Aoife, I'd prefer to wait here on my own.'

Aoife ponders a course of action for a moment. 'OK. I'll head out to the car then.'

'Thanks, but don't think you've softened me up. No radio or CDs.'

'Jesus, I think I can listen to the radio for a few minutes without the battery giving out.'

'You'll do as I say. I'm not in the mood for pushing cars, are you? There's always Ulsterbus if you have a problem with that.'

Aoife tuts, 'Christ, you're nearly as bad as Mam.'

'Huh!? Look, I'm next. Go. These things don't take long.'

'OK, mein führer. Talk to you in a bit.'

Maeve sighs and glances around at the other people waiting. She tries to look unconcerned and in control—she sometimes feels as though she is merely playing at adulthood. She doesn't want Aoife to leave, though. She is flustered. She doesn't know what to expect. The girls at work say that while it isn't the nicest of experiences, it is relatively bearable. She is going to face it with the consummate coolness that is Work Maeve—nothing fazes Work Maeve. But Work Maeve has gone A.W.O.L.

A plump, black-haired nurse with an excessively sweet voice addresses the waiting room. 'Maeve Gallagher, please.'

'Yes', Maeve answers while tentatively rising to her feet. At five feet eleven she is at least eight inches taller than the nurse. Her statuesque elegance has always singled her out.

'If you'd like to come with me this way', the nurse instructs.

Maeve complies and follows. She read somewhere that female nurses only assist in this kind of examination when the doctor is male. Suddenly unnerved, she traces a curve on her forehead with her index finger. Where is Dr Murphy? It has to be a female doctor. She has not accounted for this twist in the plot. She tries to distract herself by concentrating on the nurse, who is no more than twenty-four years old and completely without the right to be so sickeningly sweet so young. Every little detail drips from her mouth like syrup,

'My name is Clodagh. I will be assisting Doctor Paul McGrath—'

'Where is Dr Murphy?' Maeve blurts.

'She is out today. Beautiful day isn't it?'

'Yes—yes it is.' Maeve couldn't care less.

She is going through with this—no matter what.

Clodagh continues, 'I think November is the most beautiful month when it gets a good, dry run at it.'

She's so matronly and so young. She's probably been precociously married—yes, there is a wedding ring on the left hand. No doubt her mother is looking after her two oh-so-delightful children during the day. And at night she is wifey extraordinaire to her tradesman husband.

Whatever about Work Maeve, Bitch Maeve is fully present and accounted for.

Clodagh approaches a door and courteously knocks on it. After a pause, she opens it and enters the room, gesturing Maeve to follow suit.

'Doctor, this is Maeve Gallagher.'

The room is small and smells sterile, its fluorescent lights glare. The walls look harsh and unfinished: unplastered cement-grey bricks, straight out of the money-starved seventies.

'Hello, Ms Gallagher. I'm Doctor McGrath. How are you?'

He is a tall, rugged-looking man in his thirties, at once friendly and disinterested.

'I'm fine, thank you,' Maeve says.

'If you'd like to take a seat there for a second....'

'Sure, thank you very much.' Maeve sits on a green plastic chair beside an ominous-looking bed. She is facing the doctor's desk; Clodagh is standing at her right-hand side.

'OK, Ms Gallagher, today we will be taking some cell samples to evaluate your likelihood of developing Cervical Cancer. OK?'

Maeve nods confidently, 'Yes.'

He continues, 'The whole process is quite quick and there might be a small likelihood of slight discomfort. But if you have any problems—any problems at all, do let us know. We are here to make this very important examination as quick and painless as possible. OK?'

Maeve forces another nod. She is half-expecting him to offer her some duty-free. He speeds through some questions. The monosyllables of 'Yes' and 'No' are all that are required.

And then he asks, 'Are you sexually active?'

She suddenly feels as though someone has shred her into little pieces before throwing her up in the air to remain in suspension. In any other sphere she would have an answer waiting ready on her lips, but not this one. How could she not have been prepared for this question? How naïve was she? Everything is going wrong and she is not improvising well. She must look like an idiot; the pause is deafening. Both Clodagh and the doctor look up from their check-boxed inventories and settle their attention upon her.

Say something. Fuck it, say anything.

'Yes.'

'OK', the doctor says. Clodagh's gaze rests on Maeve a little too long to go unnoticed.

'That's my interrogation over,' he continues. 'I'll leave you for a few moments to get ready. Clodagh will help you.'

The doctor leaves the room, and Maeve turns to look at Clodagh. There is compassion in the young nurse's face that unsettles Maeve a little. Does she look that frightened?

'If you could take off your skirt and underwear and pop up here on the bed,' Clodagh says.

'OK,' Maeve answers while looking down at her black, figure-hugging, below-the-knee skirt and don't-even-think-about-fucking-me boots. She doesn't know where to start. The bed is to the right of where is she is seated.

Clodagh pitches in with a silly laugh. 'You'd think these beds were made for high-jumpers. You'd need a step ladder or a crate to get up on it.'

Maeve forces a smile at Clodagh's twee efforts; she cannot summon language right now.

She is going through with this—no matter what.

Seemingly out of nowhere, Clodagh pulls a curtain around Maeve and the bed, partitioning her off from the rest of the room. Maeve knows this is her cue.

She is going through with this—no matter what.

She nervously stands up, takes off her heavy black coat and places it on the chair she had been sitting on. She smoothes down her slim fitting chocolate-brown blouse, pauses, resisting the urge to clasp her neck with both hands, and takes a deep breath.

She is going through with this—no matter what.

She tries to take off her skirt. As usual it is troublesome; the zip sticks. Embarrassed, she tries to force it free, but it won't budge. She sighs heavily and then tries the gentle approach; with some persuasion it eventually gives way. Her skirt slides down her legs and she steps out of it, picks it up and places it on the same chair. She then slides her white knickers down and off and also places them on the chair. How strange she must look standing there in her boots, bare arse and fanny exposed. With self-conscious calmness she slides one black boot off after the other. They are big, clunky-looking things, comfort-oriented rather than sexy—they have a semi-lesbian look, she thinks. Standing there, she is sure she will never wear them again; they will be forever associated with this ordeal.

The whole process is timed to perfection: Clodagh peeps around the curtain just as the doctor re-enters the room with the wuffling noises of the clinic's activity at his back. The door swings itself closed behind him. The room is quiet again.

'OK, Maeve. Can you pop up onto the table now?' Clodagh asks.

'OK.'

Maeve eases herself up to sit on the bed. She looks stricken.

Clodagh quietly continues, 'OK, now if you could just lie on to your back.'

After a pause for motivation, Maeve lifts her legs awkwardly up on to the bed and lies back. Clodagh drapes a large paper towel over Maeve's stomach and thighs and adjusts the pillow to comfort her.

The doctor pulls the curtain back a little and enters this crowded, partitioned space. He moves to the bottom of the bed. His voice then booms out amid the hush:

'OK Ms. Gallagher, can you bend your knees up and let your legs flop to the side as far as you can?'

She closes her eyes for a moment and complies.

'A little more.'

Her breathing deepens. She again complies.

'Right, let's have a look.'

Nothing happens at first. Then she feels the shock of coldness; then there is a jag of pain. Terror possesses her. She again hears the little skirt rip. She again tastes the strawberries; saliva accumulates in her mouth; it's been so long since she has been haunted by this. She feels like the unconsenting subject of some gruesome, twisted Pavlovian experiment. She will never become desensitised to it.

She hears blood pulse through her brain. It has happened. *It* is unleashed back into her life proper. *It* will have to be suffered again, just like all the other times. *It* will have to be slowly but surely dealt with, again. She is defeated, again.

How can she carry on from this point? How will she get up off this cheap, plastic health service bed?

A tear emerges from her right eye, pauses upon her eyelashes, and then merges with her again, but not before Clodagh sees it.

The rest of the procedure passes by Maeve unnoticed. The apparatus is removed. The doctor makes a swift exit with some reference as to when the results will be known. Maeve eases herself up and then off the bed. She picks up her knickers and skirt and puts them on. She puts her boots on. Then she picks up her coat and moves towards the door.

Clodagh steps out from behind the curtain. She cocks her head to one side. To Maeve it seems like another well-rehearsed checklist is to be endured. She simply could not stand any more procedures. But instead, Clodagh avoids eye-contact, raises her left arm towards Maeve a little, then after a second thought drops it, and says,

'I'm sorry...'

Maeve freezes, utterly at a loss as to how this intimation should be interpreted. Tears begin to flow. She runs out of the room. She runs down the corridor past three struggling old people, almost colliding with one on a Zimmer frame; past nurses; past the reception and out through the automatic doors. She is not following any logical plan of escape. She needs fresh air. She can run the legs off herself but there is no escape. She knows it. This brings her to a halt. With a slow blinking gaze she examines the landscape of this stupid little town that she has spent so much of her life in. History is inescapable.

Aoife.

The car park is around the corner. She wipes her eyes. Luckily, she does not get big, veiny eyes when crying; Aoife will not notice.

She strides towards the car. She is going to be Work Maeve. She can do that now. Work Maeve.

As she draws close to her black BMW saloon she hears something vaguely Britney-like blaring from it. The little bitch.

On wresting the driver's door open she barks, 'What did I tell you?'

Aoife plays dumb. 'Wha'?'

'Nothing. I don't know why I bother,' Maeve says. She is too tired for issuing reprimands.

After slumping into the driver's seat and closing the door, she looks at her sister. Aoife is what she could have been: beautiful, vital and uncompromised.

Maeve turns the ignition, eases the handbrake off and is moving. She continues matter-of-factly, 'We better get you home before Josephine Stalin puts out an A.P.B. on us.'

Aoife turns the volume of the radio down. Maeve looks at her and says, 'What are you at?'

'You don't like Britney—actually you don't like music. So I turned it down.'

'Well don't bother.'

Aoife, not really comprehending, turns the music back up, louder than before. One day, she hopes, she will be just like Maeve. She smiles to herself and looks out the passenger-side window.

Leabasídhe

/Laba-Shee/
(The Fairies' Bed)

Breda Wall Ryan

IN THE TOWNLAND of Leabasídhe, a mile from the village, a *'derelict cottage on one-acre, with outline planning'* proved slow to sell. Whether this was due to the high asking price, or a stonemason's disappearance during construction of a boundary wall during the Famine, or the later spiriting away of a little girl from the cottage, was never clear. Over time, the holding's history became blurred, but the place was always considered unlucky or haunted, or by some, cursed.

When the last family moved away, the cottage lay empty for years. The thatch rotted. Rain got into the cob walls and they tumbled in on themselves. Sometimes a poor go-the-road would kindle a fire in the stone hearth and settle down to spend the night, but before the fire reddened, he felt strangely compelled to gather his bundle and billy-can and seek other shelter. A local farmer grazed his goats on the acre in the hope of establishing squatters' rights to the property. If outsiders came to look at the site, the villagers made them feel unwelcome by claiming that the land of Ireland belonged by right to the people of Ireland, and that they were being priced out of living in their native county by wealthy foreigners. If that didn't deter a buyer, they alluded to a mysterious tragic past and a history of bad luck.

When all that was left on the place was the outline of a ruin, a buyer was found for the acre; a young English couple with a child on the way, who took the locals' stories for mere idiosyncrasies. The estate agent, who was also a county councillor, expedited planning permission for a four-bedroomed hacienda-style bungalow with neo-Georgian windows and an imitation wishing-well (dry) in front. The couple moved into their new house a week after the birth of their child.

The villagers muttered among themselves against the English blow-ins in their Bungalow Bliss. The goat-farmer was forced to sell half his flock. The descendants of the man who had disappeared during construction of the famine wall expressed a belief that the English were to blame, since the Great Famine was caused by failure of the potato crop, and the Englishman Walter Raleigh had brought the potato from the New World. The English Queen Victoria had contributed a miserly five pounds to famine relief, and that grudge too they held against the English couple, as well as the present high cost of land. If the couple had not made an offer for the property, the price would have fallen and a local bid would have been successful. Mumbles against eight-hundred years of English oppression and against landgrabbers and gazumpers were heard in pub and corner shop. These opinions the villagers kept to themselves, however, and were as polite to the English couple as they were to any passing tourist. But the people of Leabasídhe were good-hearted by nature, and in time, the presence of a bonny baby melted local resentment.

Privately, the villagers thought the house an eyesore; a blot on the landscape. They nicknamed it 'The Folly'. The owners, liking the quaint name, inscribed it on the gate-post. Nobody troubled to mention their property's tragic past. No good would come of upsetting people; it might even do harm.

A year passed, then another. The blow-ins lost some of their Englishness and adopted, without realising it, an Irish outlook. It was time, they decided, to put their own stamp on the acre behind the house. They heard it called 'the *lios* field'. They asked what *lios* meant, and were much taken with the explanation of a stone circle marking a pre-historic site. A scaled-down Stonehenge behind the bungalow would be a unique architectural feature, they thought, and would dispose of the untidy mound of boulders against the ditch. Their neighbours were alarmed to see a digger and bulldozer uprooting the stones and standing them in a circle; they raised the subject of fairies and fairy-forts, but their concerns fell on English ears. To the couple, fairies were miniature do-gooders with transparent wings and magic wands, who lived in books and children's imaginations.

The workers were setting the last stone in concrete when a blast of wind rattled the windowpanes and howled like a soul in torment through a twisted blackthorn on the edge of the property. It brought on a hailstorm so heavy that it whitened the ground. Work was suspended. The wind died as suddenly as it had risen. The Englishwoman then directed the workers to uproot the blackthorn and re-plant it in the centre of the stone circle, for a natural wind-chime effect. She was delighted with her fake fairy fort and e-mailed photographs to her friends, who planned to holiday at The Folly the following summer.

But the holiday was cancelled because the child of the house, who had been as healthy as a colt from the day she was born, grew ill and listless. Doctors were baffled as to what ailed her. Tests at University Hospital yielded no clue. The water supply was tested and the Englishwoman was questioned about the child's access to poisonous substances and toxic plants. Scientists took swabs and samples. No link was found to the strange wasting disease; the child continued to fail. She suffered no pain, but her heartbroken parents saw her eyes darken and begin to eat up her wan face. She stopped smiling. They gave up hope.

Then two things happened at once: The Englishman was transferred to his company's headquarters near Cambridge, and the Englishwoman decided she would take in lodgers, for the security a man in the house provided and to make extra money to cover the expense of their upcoming move with the sick child back to England.

But before her 'Rooms To Let' advertisement appeared in the

post-office window or the newspaper, she received a phone call from the landlady of a boarding-house, asking if she could take in a lodger for a few weeks, as her own establishment was full. Amazed at her good fortune, she agreed at once.

Next day, she waved her husband off and was about to go indoors, when she heard a drone from the direction of the cross-roads. The drone grew to a growl and within minutes, a ten-horse-power motorbike roared into the drive. The rider, with the wind in his hair, skidded to a halt. The wheels spat gravel against her legs. She had second thoughts about taking a lodger, but his smile dispelled her misgivings. His gaze was forthright. His eyes seemed familiar. They were a flat blue-green, and expressionless. She could not think of whom they reminded her. He dismounted, swung his pannier-bags onto his shoulder and bowed slightly to the Englishwoman before following her indoors.

After sundown each evening, the biker drew his chair close to the sickly child on the living room couch and began to enthral her with stories. His stories never varied in any detail. Soon, the child began to mouth the words as he spoke, and they recited the stories together. At first, she had begged, 'Tell me a story.' But later, she pleaded, 'Tell *our* story.' Then man and child sat with their heads together, and the woman listened entranced to the soft slippery slide of syllables sounding out tales older than time.

'*Long, long ago in the time of No-Time, in the land of Leabasídhe, where featherbedded fairy-folks hide from the eyebright daylight of Earthworld, deep in the Otherworld Underworld beyond the wide Western Ocean…*'

The Englishwoman saw that though the child grew weaker by the minute and would soon be lost to her, the biker's stories brought a strange light to the child's eyes. They chanted of '*Owl-white night birds and midnight puffballs and a No-Time Otherworld behind doors that open in the sheltered hillside, where no door appears in Now-Time; the door to Tír na nÓg, Land of Forever Young.*' The biker's haunting refrain punctuated the rhyme and rhythm and melody of the incantation:

'*See the door! Come, step with me through the door!*'

The Englishwoman worried that the tales frightened the child; her small body grew weaker and her eyes larger with every telling. But then she saw the child's happiness and the bond the stories forged between child and storyteller and decided they did no harm.

Tales of mortals enticed through the portals of Otherworld and lost forever to Earthworld helped the Englishwoman to weep for the child she was losing. She asked her lodger to write down the stories so that she could read them to the child in the daytime, when he was away. He grew agitated, and refused. She suggested that she record the words herself if he would speak slowly, but to this he replied that he made the stories up as he went along and could not afterwards remember them. The woman knew that was a lie; he had told the same stories night after night. With every telling, more of the child's strength ebbed from her and they recited faster, in order to reach the end before she had to lie back, exhausted. So, unbeknownst to her lodger, the woman wrote the stories while he told them.

'*Long, long ago, in the land of Leabasídhe, a hungry mortal saw a hare hiding in the portal of the Lios. He snared the hare and killed it. The fairies were stirred to anger, but because of his hunger, they pardoned him. Next, he ripped branches from a fairy thorn and lit a fire in the Lios, and set the hare over the fire to roast. Seeing their Lios desecrated and their thorn torn, the fairymen mounted their white horses and rode out against him. Out from a door in the stone-built famine wall they thundered. Harness all a-jangle, they surrounded him. He felt the blast of a fairy wind and a shower of icy hailstones doused the forbidden fire...*'

Fast as the tales tumbled from the lips of the biker and the mesmerised child, the Englishwoman captured every word. When words fell hard as drumming hooves, her pen sped across the page. The biker's voice fell to the whisper of a breeze through a beech and the child's voice strengthened. The woman increased her writing pace and did not notice the man's loss or the child's gain. Their words became a flutter of dry leaves danced by a cold wind, and she wrote on and the story of the mortal who stepped through the enchanted door segued into a tale that was more recent, though yet of a time long past.

'Long, long ago in Now-Time, in Leabasídhe of Earthworld, above the Otherworld Featherbed of Fairy-folks, lived a mortal family who lost their girlchild. She was walking home from school. By the postman's gate she stroked his black cat. He purred his deepdown, throat-deep contentment. On she went, piping trills to thrush and robin. The postman's wife watched her feet flash the steps of a reel; so feather-light on tip-toe she wouldn't break the skin on water. Around the bend of the road she toe-tapped. Home was but a short step away, but the girlchild's dance didn't cover that short step. Never again was she seen by mortal man.

'When the sun hung above the mountain ash, the mother felt uneasy. Down the bohereen she went, searching for her girlchild. She told herself the reasons why her child might be late-coming: The teacher had detained her. She was playing at the crossroads. Time had passed unnoticed. Then the church-bell chimed, without sight or sign of the girlchild. The mother lifted the baby on her hip and went again to the roadside, there to wait stock-still in fear and anger. Fear and anger were her feelings when she broke herself a hazel to switch the legs off the girlchild, for the heartache she had caused her. All manner of calamity then filled her imagining. She threw away the hazel-switch and willed her mind to stillness. She stopped herself from thinking then at all.

'Behind the cottage was an acre bounded along one side by a famine wall. Under a stone circle at the centre of the field lay Leabasídhe, feather-bed of Fairyfolk, Fairy Fort gateway from Earthworld to Otherworld, until the day the mother hired a tractor-man to push the stones back against the ditch and level the ground. She believed neither in fairies nor their forts, and cared nothing that Fairies might believe in her.

'That May evening was still and sunny. If the girlchild had come home, she would have been helping her mother to redden the earth and plant out seedlings. The mother fixed that tranquil scene in her mind, and wondered if the child was staying away because the work of turning the sod was heavy. She hoped it was so. She stood by the gate in the warm scent of evening until a black cloud blocked the sun. A squall sprang up. It whipped up dust-devils; they whirled around the mother, stinging her bare legs and making her eyes water. She heard a hum that she took to be a lorry lumbering up the hill from the crossroads, and her heart rose at the thought that when *it turned the corner, she would see her girlchild in the cab beside the driver; the light of her life would be home. The sound drew closer; she knew it for the galloping of horses. She prayed her child would not be trampled, if the child was on the road. Onward the hooves came; they turned the corner. Still she saw no horses. Then a terrible fear gripped her. The hooves thundered past the spot where she stood. Sparks flew where iron-shod hooves struck stone. The riders' shouts filled her ears. She heard the slap of leather on withers, the silvery jangle of harness; hard-galloping, rough-riding, heaving horse-herd; neighing and whickering. She felt the air shift with their passing, and smelled horse-sweat. But she saw no horses. Then she knew her girlchild was lost to her.'*

The biker broke out in a sweat from the effort of telling the story. Each word the Englishwoman penned snatched another ounce of his strength. She did not notice, or see, health return to the child's pale cheeks and her limbs grow smooth and plump.

'That evening, the girlchild's father found his wife demented. He alerted the guards and a search-party was got up, and a doctor sent for, and everything possible was done to lift the family's distress. Nightwalking men, poachers, and badger-baiters drove themselves ragged with searching. When one collapsed, another took over. They searched every inch of ground, every rock and bush, every well and stream and boghole; in forked oaks and foxes' dens. But they found no trace of the girlchild, then or ever.'

The child finished the story alone in a clear, silvery sing-song.

'She was away with the Fairies.' She swung her legs over the side of the bed and sat, gathering strength.

The Englishwoman set down the last word of the story and flexed her fingers. She saw the biker lurch to his feet. Alarmed at his laboured breathing, she told him to sit while she called a doctor, but he staggered to the blackthorn in the imitation fairy fort, plucked a handful of bitter green sloes and chewed them without wincing. Then he grabbed his pannier-bag. He grew feebler; shuffling like a man with crumbling bones. The weight of the bag was too much for him, so he dumped it at the foot of the famine wall, struggled onto the saddle of his motorbike and rode away.

A sudden hailstorm drove the Englishwoman indoors. A gale of wind sliced hail into her face and rattled the windowpanes. During the night, she heard a loud rumble, but she was afraid to investigate in the darkness. Next morning, the boundary wall was down and a jumble of bones, brittle and decayed, protruded from the rubble, along with a couple of giant puffballs. She notified the Guards. They believed she had discovered the remains of a man and a little girl who had disappeared from Leabasídhe a hundred years apart. The evidence suggested they had both become entombed in the same hollow section of stonework. She mentioned the biker-lodger to the Guards, but not wanting to be thought foolish, she said nothing about his stories. During his stay, she had called the lodger Mr. Ferry, thinking that was his name. He had not corrected her, but the Guards decided she had been mistaken. Because his bags had disappeared, they thought he had returned and might have seen the wall collapse. They searched, but neither man nor bike was found.

Thoughts of the little girl buried alive inside the wall haunted the Englishwoman. She could not bear to stay any longer at the site of such horror and decided to join her husband at once. Before the day was out, she had loaded the car with what she could carry and made arrangements with a removals firm and an estate agent. She and the child left for England by ferry the following afternoon.

When her car drove away, the forensics team heard what sounded like a great herd of horses galloping past. They stopped working to watch. But they saw no horses. Being scientists, they looked for a logical explanation.

The winters since have been hard on the place. Facia and soffit are rotten. Slates have slipped and starlings nest under the roof. The bottoms of the doors are gone. The grass in the acre is long and full of weeds; they say it's gone too bitter even for goats.

And a young lad from the village got a stab of a blackthorn when he was retrieving a football from the twisted tree in the fake fairy fort. Gangrene set in. They've had to amputate the arm. Please God, that'll be the end of it.

Please God.

And the Fairymen.

Biographies

❀

Georgina Eddison is a psychotherapist who was born and reared in Dublin. She has published poetry in *Broadsheet*, *Cyphers*, *The Sunday Tribune* and *The Shop*. She has also published several short stories and is currently working on a novel.

William Collinson was brought up by a pack of badgers in the New Forest. A thoughtful child, he would often write epic poetry on pieces of bark, before eating them, and then paint himself with mud. Nobody knows how he got onto the course at Trinity, but everyone's too afraid to challenge him about it. If you see him in the street, offer him raw meat and back away slowly.

Kamala Nair was born in 1981. She studied English Literature at Wellesley College and Oxford University. She is currently working on a novel and a collection of poetry.

Sabina Conerney was born in Dublin in 1981. She graduated from Trinity College, Dublin in 2004 with a degree in English and History. She loves to write stories, poetry and plays and draws her inspiration from the ordinary person on the street who, she maintains, is leading a not-so-ordinary life.

Geraldine McMenamin was born in London and brought up in Dublin. She has lived and worked in hot places. Currently in the process of finishing her first novel, she is thrilled to be published in the anthology.

James D. Sumner: Fun-loving Aquarian, G.S.O.H, W.L.T.M. agent or publisher for mutual stimulation. Arguably the most brilliant unpublished writer of his generation, he likes travel and sport.

Kevin Kiely was born in Warrenpoint, Co. Down; has lived, worked and studied in England, Spain and the United States. He is the author of 'Quintesse' (St. Martin's Press, New York and Co-Op Books, Dublin), 'Mere Mortals' (Odell&Adair/Poolbeg, Dublin),

'Plainchant for a Sundering' (Lapwing, Belfast) and 'Breakfast with Sylvia' (Lagan, Belfast). His radio plays include 'Multiple Indiscretions' and 'Children of No Importance' broadcast by RTÉ. He is the recipient of six Arts Council Bursary Awards in Literature and Honorary Fellow-in-Writing (University of Iowa), editor/literary critic and, is currently completing a biography of Francis Stuart, as well as working on 'A Horse Called El Dorado' (released September), the first of three novels for young people.

Brandon M. Crose lives in Boston, Massachusetts. This is his first publication; a three-month gig as an online sex columnist notwithstanding. He writes fiction and drama, and is currently finishing a novel about ice cream truck drivers, from which 'The Entertainer' is an excerpt.

Playwright and actor **Eithne McGuinness** wrote *Typhoid Mary* for the Dublin Fringe Theatre Festival 1997. It was short-listed for the P.J.O'Connor Awards and broadcast by RTÉ Radio in 1998. In 2004, the play was performed in the New Theatre in Temple Bar with a subsequent national tour. Eithne has been invited to perform *Typhoid Mary* in the Irish Historical Society in New York in 2005. *Limbo* was written for the Dublin Fringe Theatre Festival in 2000; the play was revived in 2001 with support from the Arts Council and the City Arts Centre. As an actor, Eithne has worked with The Abbey Theatre, Passion Machine and Calypso among others. She played Gracie Tracey on *Glenroe* and Sister Clementine in *The Magdalen Sisters* (Golden Lion).

Roisín Boyd is a television and radio journalist who lives in Dublin. She has reported from Asia, Africa and Latin America; including Vietnam, Rwanda, Somalia, Cuba and most recently the Democratic Republic of Congo.

John Durnin is twenty-two years old. He studied English and Art History at Villanova University, and hopes to pursue a PhD in English after spending a year in Kyoto. He is currently writing a novel.

Patrick Finnegan is twenty-three years old, and comes from County Armagh in Northern Ireland. He has a BEng in Computer Science from Queen's University Belfast, and currently works in an investment bank. He is currently working on his novel-in-progress, 'What Remains'.

Breda Wall Ryan's stories have been shortlisted for a Hennessy Award and the Davy Byrne Award and have been published in *New Irish Writing* and in *Moments: Short Stories by Irish Women Writers*. She is working on a novel and a short story collection.